Joshua Toulmin

A Review of the Life, Character and Writings of the Rev. John Biddle, M.A.

Who was banished to the Isle of Scilly in the protectorate of Oliver Cromwell

Joshua Toulmin

A Review of the Life, Character and Writings of the Rev. John Biddle, M.A.
Who was banished to the Isle of Scilly in the protectorate of Oliver Cromwell

ISBN/EAN: 9783337410889

Printed in Europe, USA, Canada, Australia, Japan

Cover: Foto ©Raphael Reischuk / pixelio.de

More available books at **www.hansebooks.com**

A

REVIEW

OF THE

LIFE, CHARACTER AND WRITINGS

OF THE

Rev. *JOHN BIDDLE, M. A.*

WHO WAS BANISHED TO THE ISLE OF SCILLY, IN THE
PROTECTORATE OF OLIVER CROMWELL.

By JOSHUA TOULMIN, A.M.

───────

*Others had trial of cruel mockings and scourgings; yea,
moreover of bonds and imprisonment: of whom the
world was not worthy.*

───────

LONDON:

PRINTED FOR J. JOHNSON, BOOKSELLER, N°. 72,
ST. PAUL'S CHURCH-YARD.

MDCCLXXXIX.

PREFACE.

THE character brought forward in the following Memoirs was, more than an hundred years ago, a character of celebrity, at home and abroad. The queſtions concerning the doctrine of the Trinity, that have been lately agitated, properly render it an object of curioſity to the preſent age; for Mr. Biddle was the Father of the *Engliſh Unitarians.*

But his hiſtory is a more important ſubject of attention, on account of the ſevere perſecutions he ſuſtained, and the amiable, venerable piety he exemplified. Memoirs of ſuch as have

diſplayed

difplayed fingular virtues, and fupported fingular fufferings, for what
they deemed divine truth, will always be ufeful; to fhew the power of
religious principle, and to convince
men, that true piety is not peculiar
to thofe who embrace a particular
Creed, but the genuine fruit of thofe
principles, which are common to all
Chriftians.

From thefe views is the Author
induced to lay before the public the
life of Mr. BIDDLE, which he pre-
fumes cannot fail to prove, to the
candid and ferious mind, inftructive
and edifying. To the attention of
fuch, and to the blefling of God, he
would humbly commend it.

Taunton, March 22, 1789.

A

A

R E V I E W

OF THE

LIFE, CHARACTER, and WRITINGS

OF THE

Rev. JOHN BIDDLE, A. M.

SECTION I.

The *Birth*, *Education*, and *First* **Settle-**
ment, of MR. JOHN BIDDLE.

EXCELLENCE and merit of charác-
ter are independent of the circumftances of rank and place : yet the mind is
gratified by the information, that can be
procured, concerning the family and birth
of fuch as have diftinguifhed themfelves by
their virtues, or gained in any walk of life
peculiar reputation.

B   The

The good man, whofe character and writings will be reviewed in the following pages, derived no luftre from the honours of his defcent; nor can his family be traced back beyond the name and rank of his immediate progenitor. He was the fon of Mr. *Edward Biddle*, a woollen draper, at *Wotton-under-edge*, in the county of *Gloucefter*; a perfon whofe circumftances were not affluent, but who fupported his family with virtuous reputation, and a credit rather above his rank. His fon, Mr. *John Biddle*, the fubject of thefe memoirs, was born in that town, in the year 1615.

He received his claffical education at the free-fchool, in the fame place. He was not ten years of age, when his promifing abilities, and the opening bloffoms of genius and probity, drew on him the notice of his neighbours, and fpread his fame through the country. *George*, lord *Berkley*, who was a munificent patron of genius and learning, conferred on him, amongft other fcholars, an exhibition of ten pounds per annum; but with this mark of diftinction,
that

that he beſtowed it on the young *Biddle* at a more early period than he was accuſtomed to grant this donation.

Our youth, animated by this encouragement, purſued his ſtudies with new vigour. His emulation was kindled ; ſo that, with eaſe, he not only ſurpaſſed his ſchool-fellows of the ſame rank; " but, in time, out-ran his inſtructions, and became tutor to himſelf."

In this period of his life, he gave ſeveral particular ſpecimens of the pregnancy of his parts, and his proficiency in learning. On the death of a ſchool-fellow of high rank, he compoſed an elaborate oration in *Latin*, which he recited before a full auditory. He alſo tranſlated into Engliſh verſe, the Eclogues of *Virgil*, and the two firſt Satires of *Juvenal*. We are led to entertain an high opinion of the execution of theſe juvenile performances, from this circumſtance, that they were afterwards printed at London in 1634, with the approbation of ſome learned men ; and dedicated

to

to *John Smith*, Efq. of *Nibley*, in the county of *Gloucefter*.

But notwithftanding the rapid and fingular progrefs which he made in claffical learning, he was through different caufes, detained at fchool till he was about feventeen years of age. In 1632 he was fent to the univerfity of *Oxford*, and was admitted a ftudent in *Magdalen Hall*. Here he profecuted his ftudies with great affiduity and increafing fame : and was efteemed as doing honour to that feminary. It feems, that he now difcovered not only a brilliancy of parts, but a peculiar liberality and independence of mind; for we are told, " he " did fo philofophize, that it might be ob- " ferved, he was determined more by rea- " fon, than authority : however, in divine " things he did not diffent much from the " common doctrine." Of this, it feems, that a little piece he wrote againft dancing furnifhed proof.

On the 23d of *June*, 1638, he took the degree of Batchelor of Arts; and with reputation, both for learning and prudence,
filled

filled the poft of a tutor in the Univerfity.
On the 20th of *May*, 1641, the degree of
Mafter of Arts was conferred upon him
with great applaufe. Before this he had received an invitation to be mafter of the
fchool in his native town, which he declined. But the reputation, which procured
this offer, directed the views of the magiftrates of *Gloucefter* to him: as his having
refufed it, left him free to attend to other
overtures. In 1641, in confequence of
ample recommendations, from the principal perfons in the Univerfity, he was elect-
ed mafter of the free-fchool of *Crifps*, in
the city of *Gloucefter*. This choice was accompanied with earneft importunities. He
accepted the invitation, and on his going
to fettle in this poft; he was met at his approach to the city, by the magiftrates, and
was received with honourable expreffions
of joy and refpect.

In this department he anfwered the ex-
pectations which had been formed of him.
His fkill and faithfulnefs were eminent.
They, who could commit their fons to his

tuition,

tuition, congratulated themſelves on their felicity. Hence, though the fixed ſalary was not great, the gratuities of parents made the emoluments of it conſiderable.

SECTION

SECTION II.

The *Freedom* of his *Religious Enquiries*.

THE circumftances of Mr. *Biddle*'s fituation were truly inviting, and opened to him a pleafing profpect of ufefulnefs and felicity. But his happinefs in it was of fhort continuance. The love of money had not corrupted his mind: nor could the views of intereft divert his attention from objects of a different nature. That freedom of enquiry which he had difcovered in his philofophical and academical ftudies, was now directed to the fubjects of religion. " Having laid afide the impedi-
" ments of prejudice, he gave himfelf li-
" berty, we are told, to try all things, that
" he might hold faft that which is good."

To adopt the obfervations of a great writer, as pertinent here, as they are juft in themfelves. " Since the underftandings of men are fimilar to one another, (at leaft

B 4   fo

so much, as that no perfon can ferioufly maintain that *two and two* make *five*,) did they actually read only the fame things, and had they no previous knowledge to miflead them, they could not but draw the fame general conclufions from the fame expreffions. But one man having formed an hypothefis from reading the fcriptures, another, who follows him, ftudies that hypothefis, and refines upon it, and another again refines upon him; till in time, the fcriptures themfelves are little read by any of them: and are never looked into but with minds prepoffeffed with the notions of others concerning them. At the fame time feveral other *original readers* and thinkers, having formed as many other hypothefes, each of them a little different from all the reft, and all of them being improved upon by a fucceffion of partifans, each of whom contributes to widen the difference; at laft no religions whatever, the moft diftinct originally, are more different from one another, than the various forms of *one* and the fame religion.

" To

" To remedy this inconvenience, we muft go back to firft principles. We muft begin again, each of us carefully ftudying the fcriptures for ourfelves, without the help of commentators, comparing one part with another. And when our minds fhall, by this means, have been expofed to the fame influences, we fhall think and feel in the fame manner.

" Were it poffible for a number of perfons to make but an effay towards complying with this advice, by confining themfelves for the compafs of a fingle year, to the daily reading of the fcriptures, without any other religious books whatever, I am perfuaded, that, notwithftanding their previous differences, they would think much better of one another than they had done before. They would all have more nearly the fame general ideas of the contents, and of the chief articles of chriftian faith and duty. By reading the whole themfelves, they could hardly avoid receiving the deepeft impreffions of the certainty, and importance of the great and *leading principles*;

thofe

thofe which they would find moft frequently
and earneftly inculcated : and their particular opinions having come lefs frequently
in view, would be lefs obftinately retained.
It was in this manner, I can truly fay, that
I formed the moft diftinguifhing of my opinions in religion *."

In this manner it appears, that Mr. *Biddle*
formed thofe fentiments, by which he was
afterwards diftinguifhed. He gave the
Holy Scriptures a diligent reading : and
made ufe of no other rule to determine
controverfies about religion, than the *fcriptures* ; and of no other *authentic interpreter*,
if a fcruple arofe, concerning the fenfe of
the fcriptures, than *reafon* †.

This method of fettling the mind on
points of religious enquiry, he ftrongly recommended to others. " If thou, Chriftian
reader, doft from thy heart afpire to the
knowledge of God, and his fon *Jefus
Chrift*, wherein, as Chrift himfelf teftifieth,

---

* Priestley's *Confiderations on differences of Opinion in Religion,* p. 25, 26.

† Life, p. 4. and Teftimonies, p. 82. 12mo.

eternal

eternal life doth confift, John 17. 3. fetch
not the beginning thereof either from *So-*
cinus (a man otherwife of great underftanding in the myftery of the Gofpel) nor
from his adverfaries; but being mindful
of thofe words, Luke x. 22. *None knoweth*
who the Son is but the Father; and who
the Father is, but the Son, and he to whom
the Son will reveal him : lay afide, for a
while, controverfial writings, together with
thofe prejudicate opinions that have been
inftilled into thine unwary underftanding,
and clofely applying thyfelf to the fearch
of the New Covenant, moft ardently im-
plore the grace of Chrift, that he would
be pleafed to manifeft himfelf and the
Father to thee; and make no doubt but
the true light will at length illuminate the
eyes of thy mind, that thou mayeft walk
in the way that leadeth unto life *."

So faithfully did Mr. *Biddle* himfelf purfue this plan of inveftigating divine truth,
that he derived all his learning in matters

* See preface to a Difcourfe concerning the peace
and concord of the church, p. 2, 3, 4,

of

of religion from the affiduous ftudy of the
fcriptures, efpecially of the New Teftament; with which he was fo converfant,
that he retained it all in his memory *ver-*
batim, not only in Englifh but in Greek;
as far as the fourth chapter of the *Revela-*
tions. The natural confequence and advantage of this perfect and exact knowledge
of the New Teftament, it is obvious, muft
have been a comprehenfive view of its
contents, a familiar acquaintance with its
language and phrafeology, fo as readily to
compare it together as it occurred to his
recollection from different places, and a
command of the full connexion in which
any paffage ftands.

It alfo appears, that when he firft began
to purfue religious enquiries, and to form
his fentiments for himfelf, he did not, as
many have, immediately read the firft writers
of the Chriftian Church. For, in a piece
he afterwards publifhed, having quoted fome
paffages from *Eufebius*, he adds, " How
plainly now doth *Eufebius*, by the paffages
cited out of him, give atteftation to what
I hold

I hold touching the nature of the Ho.y Spirit, fo that one would think I learned it from him ; whereas I knew not either of his book, or of what was delivered therein, a great while after I had delivered my opinion *."

The tract where he thus expreffes him-felf, fhews indeed, that he afterwards care-fully examined the fathers, to afcertain their fentiments concerning the One God : but it likewife proves, that he had a low opinion of their judgment, or of the weight of their teftimony, which he ufed merely as an *argumentum ad hominem*.

It may be alledged, as a clear proof of the independence of Mr. *Biddle*'s mind, and of his freedom from the influence of human authority, that he had read no *So-cinian* writer when he fettled his judgment concerning the doctrine of the Trinity; though he afterwards looked into the *Polifh* writers of that clafs.

---

* The Teftimonies, p. 7. or the fame in Uni-tarian Tracts, v. 1, p. 27.

It

It is remarkable, that alſo the candid and excellent Dr. *Lardner*, who amongſt the writers of this century, takes a lead on the Unitarian ſide, declares the ſame of himſelf. "I muſt acknowledge that I have not been greatly converſant with the writers of that denomination, (i. e. the Socinians.) I have never read *Crellius de uno Deo Patre:* though I believe it to be a very good book. There is alſo in our own language a collection of Unitarian Tracts in two or three quartos. But I am not acquainted with it. Nor can I remember that I ever looked into it. I have formed my ſentiments upon the ſcriptures, and by reading ſuch commentators, chiefly, as are in the beſt repute. I may add, that the reading of the antient writers of the church has been of uſe to confirm me, and to aſſiſt me in clearing difficulties *."

Whether

* A Letter on the *Logos*, written in the year 1730, p. 55. Since the above was drawn up, the author has received a letter from a learned and judicious correſpondent, a Miniſter of an Unitarian Society

Whether thefe eminent and able perfons, *Biddle* and *Lardner*, attained to the knowledge of the truth, every one muft judge
for himfelf. But this is certain, a method
more proper in itfelf, or more promifing
of fuccefs, could not be adopted, than a
diligent application to the only authoritative
fource of true information on the fubject of
their enquiry.

To return to Mr. *Biddle*. The temper,
with which he profecuted his enquiries, was
fuitable to the nature and importance of
his refearches.

Society amongft the *Baptifts* in *Holland*, who fays
the fame of himfelf. " I was in the fame cafe with
Dr. *Lardner*, and could ufe his words. (See LIND-
SEY's *Two Differtations*, p. 43., To this time, I
never had read *Socinus* or Socinian writers, before
the works of *Lindfey*, by which my own fentiments
are enlarged. I read, before the year 1775, no
commentators, no antient writers of the church.
A year's ftudying the Old and New Teftament led
me into the way of truth. My honoured mafter
was an *Arian*, rather *Clarkian*. More than one of
my friends, after my example, found the truth by
reading alone the fcriptures."

As

As the lucrative profpects of his fituation did not feduce him into an indifference
to the knowledge of divine truth; fo, we
are told, that he was influenced in his pur-
fuit of it, not by a vain curiofity, but by
" the love of Chrift, who is truth and life."
His diligent reading of the fcriptures was
accompanied with fervent prayers for the
divine illumination. The manner and ftrain
of his addrefs, prefixed to his *Twelve Arguments*, is a fpecimen and proof of that
ferious fpirit which he poffeffed; and of
the pious convictions under which his refearches were conducted.

" Chriftian reader, I befeech thee," he
writes, " as thou tendereft thy falvation, that
thou wouldft thoroughly examine the following difputation in the fear of God, confidering how much his glory is concerned
therein *."

Thefe arguments were not offered to the
public with a decifive tone, and as the
refult of a fixed determination on the point,

* Twelve Arguments. The preface, or Unitarian
Tracts, v. 1. p. 16.

which

which is difcuffed in them; but with the avowed defign of calling forth fome able and learned perfons to inveftigate the queftion, and refolve his doubts.

" The author," he fays, " hath a long time waited upon learned men, for a fatisfactory anfwer to thefe arguments; but hath received none. His hopes are, that the publifhing of them will be a means to produce it; that he may receive fatisfaction, and others may be held no longer in fufpenfe, who are in travail with an earneft expectation as well as he *."

Upon Mr. *Biddle*'s examination of the Holy Scriptures, it appeared to him, that the common doctrine concerning the Trinity was not well founded in revelation, much lefs in reafon. Being as communicative of his fentiments, when occafion offered, as he was free in his enquiries, he fpake of his doubts without referve, and opened his reafons for calling the truth of that doctrine into queftion. This difcovery of his thoughts foon alarmed the

* Twelve Arguments, the preface, p. 4, 5.

fears,

fears, and inflamed the fpirits of fome zealots. The charge of herefy was raifed againft him, and he was fummoned before the magiftrates; to whom he exhibited, on the point about which he was accufed, the following Confeffion of Faith, viz.

1. I believe that there is but one infinite and almighty effence, called GOD.

2. I believe, that as there is but one infinite and almighty effence, fo there is but one perfon in that effence.

3. I believe that our Saviour Jefus Chrift is truly God, by being truly, really and properly united to the only perfon of the infinite and almighty effence.

This confeffion was made *May* 2, 1644. It failed of giving fatisfaction to the magiftrates, who urged him to be more explicit concerning the plurality of perfons in the divine effence. Accordingly, about four days after, knowing that the word *Perfon*, when afcribed to the Divine Being, was ufed in various fenfes, both by the antient fathers and modern writers, he con-

feffed,

feffed, that there were three in that one
divine effence, commonly termed perfons.

"By this it appears, obferves the author
of his life, that how diftinct foever might
be his conceptions concerning the Trinity,
yet he was not determinate enough in his
expreffing of that matter, as he became not
long after." Mr. Biddle's fecond confeffion was indeed clearly contradictory to
the firft which he exhibited. But candor
will make every allowance for a man, probably intimidated by the profpect of a
prifon; whofe mind was not fully made up
on a queftion involved in the intricacies of
fcholaftic controverfy, and whofe holy fortitude was as yet in the firft feeble ftage of
its exercife.

SECTION

SECTION III.

His Tract entitled Twelve Arguments.

IN whatever darkness or ambiguity the language of Mr. *Biddle* was involved, when he was summoned a second time, to make a confession of his faith; it reflects honour on his sincerity and fortitude, that, afterwards, he expressed himself with greater clearness and precision. Instead of desisting from enquiries which had already threatened, nay endangered, his security and peace, he resumed them with new vigour, and with a serious spirit of piety and earnest prayer to Almighty God for his assistance, he pursued his examination of the scriptures, on the point in dispute, with greater attention and care.

" A love of sacred truth is hardly consistent with an absolute indifference about its reception in the world." The mind of Mr. Biddle, it appears, was as act've to

impart,

impart, as it was folicitous to gain the knowledge of divine things. His refolution to aver and communicate his conceptions kept pace with the convictions which he obtained on the points he inveftigated. For as he proceeded in his refearches, he conferred with his friends on the fubject and refult of his enquiries, and freely opened his mind on the queftions concerning one God and three perfons.

Amongft other communications, that he made to his acquaintance was a paper, entitled, " *Twelve Arguments* drawn out of the fcripture, wherein the commonly received opinion touching the Deity of the Holy Spirit is clearly and fully refuted." Thefe arguments were drawn up in the form of fo many fyllogifms, and each was illuftrated and fupported by diftinct explanations and reafonings.

To many, who with the author do not embrace the common doctrine of the Trinity, his arguments under thofe logical propofitions, will appear to reft more on the found of words, than to be derived from

a liberal

a liberal interpretation of fcripture, and an enlarged acquaintance with its idioms and language.

They all proceed on this principle, and are meant to eſtabliſh it, viz. that the holy Spirit is a perſon or intelligent Being. The fame opinion of the diſtinct perſonality of the Holy Spirit has been advanced and defended by confiderable writers *, who have denied his Deity. But the moſt full and candid view of the language of fcripture, on this head, has been given us by the excellent Dr. *Lardner* †.

The point elucidated and argued in this tract is, " that by the words, the *Spirit,* " the *Spirit of God,* and the *Spirit of the* " *Lord,* which occur in the Old Teſta-

---

* See Dr. Scott's Demonſtration of the Scripture Doctrine of the Trinity, and an Appeal to the Common Senſe of Chriſtian People.

† A Letter concerning the Logos, written in the year 1730, the firſt poſtfcript. The point has been very lately difcuſſ'd, and clofely argued in an ingenious little tract, entitled, " The Imperſonality of the Holy Spirit. Printed for John Maſſom, 1787."

" ment,

" ment, is meant, not a being or an intelli-
" gent agent; but a power, a gift, a favour,
" a blessing: and that by the phrases, the
" *Spirit*, the *Holy* **Spirit**, the *Holy* *Ghost*,
" the *Spirit of* **God**, the *Spirit of* *Truth*,
" the *Comforter*, in the New Testament, is
" also meant a gift, or the plentiful ef-
" fusion of miraculous and spiritual gifts."
Were it not to incur the censure of dog-
matising and using too decisive a tone, one
would be tempted to pronounce this piece of
Dr. Lardner's satisfactory and unanswerable.

One remark of the great author deserves
particular attention, and carries great force
with it. It is this: " That there is not in
the Acts of the Apostles, or in any other
book of the New Testament, any account
of the appearance and manifestation of a
great agent or person, after our Saviour's
ascension; therefore no such thing was pro-
mised or intended by our Saviour, or expected by the Apostles, who could not but
know his meaning."

This fact seems to have escaped the attention of those, who have argued for the perfonality

fonality of the Holy Spirit: nor have they
made due allowance for the ftyle of the
Holy Scriptures, in which it is not uncom-
mon to perfonify many things, to which we
do not afcribe intelligence. In this view
the expreffions concerning charity, fin and
death, are as explicit and ftrong, as, any
that are applied to the Holy Spirit.

As to our Lord's language in particular,
it is on this point, a very pertinent and fenfible obfervation of a great writer : " That
it is lefs extraordinary that the figure called
perfonification, fhould be made ufe of by
him here, as the peculiar prefence of the
fpirit of God, which was to be evidenced
by the power of working miracles, was to
fucceed in the place of a real perfon, viz.
himfelf, and to be to them what he himfelf
had been, viz. their advocate, comforter,
and guide *."

It was, it fhould feem, a long time, before the idea of the perfonality of the Holy
Spirit became a fixed opinion, and an arti-

* PRIESTLEY's Hiftory of the Corruptions of
Chriftianity, vol. i. part 2. § 7. p. 88.

cle

cle of faith. For, as it is modeſtly expreſ-
ſed by Dr. *Lardner*, on a review of the
chriſtian writers of the firſt three centuries,
" it is probable, that the doctrine of the
Trinity, which is now commonly received,
and which is ſo much diſliked by many,
was not formed all at once, but was the
work of ſeveral ages *."

To return to Mr. *Biddle*'s tract. To it
are ſubjoined expoſitions of ſome particular
texts, the elucidation of which is connected
with the queſtions diſcuſſed in the *Twelve
Arguments*. It may be uſeful, and acceptable, if we ſelect one or two of theſe expoſitions.

For inſtance, 1 John 5, 7. *And theſe
three are one.* Mr. *Biddle* waves ſpeaking
of the ſuſpectedneſs of the text, but obſerves : " That it would have been hard, if
not impoſſible, (had not men been precor-
rupted) that it ſhould ever come into any
one's head to imagine, that this phraſe, *are*

---

* The ſame, p. 90. and *Lardner*'s Letter on the
Logos, p. 107.

one,

one, did fignify, *have one effence:* fince fuch
an expofition is not only contrary to common fenfe, but alfo to other places of fcripture, wherein this kind of fpeaking perpetually fignifieth an union in confent and
agreement, or the like, but never an union
in effence. To omit other facred writers,
this very Apoftle in his Gofpel, ch. xvii.
verfes 11, 21, 22, 23, ufeth this fame expreffion fix times, intimating no other but
an union of agreement: yea, in verfe 8.
of this very chapter in his epiftle, he ufeth it
in the fame fenfe. For though the expreffion
varieth fomewhat in the ordinary Greek
Teftament, in that the prepofition *εν* is prefixed, (although the Complutenfian Bible
readeth it, εις το εν ωσιν, in both verfes) yet
is the fenfe the fame ; this latter being
fpoken after the Hebrew idiom, the former
according to the ordinary phrafe : for con-
firmation whereof fee *Matt.* xix. ver. 5
and 6. together in the original. Wherefore this expreffion ought to be rendered
alike in both verfes ; as the former interpreters did it, though the latter interpreters in
v. 8.

v. 8. have rendered it *agree in one*, putting the glofs inftead of the tranflation *."

On *Ifaiah* vi. 9, 10. Mr. *Biddle* obferves, that it is argued that the Holy Spirit is the Lord; becaufe on comparing this text with Acts xxviii. 25, 26, 27. that which in *Ifaiah* is attributed to the Lord, is in the *Acts* afcribed to the Holy Spirit. Which kind of arguing, though it be very frequent with them, is yet very frivolous: for at this rate, he adds, I may alfo conclude, that becaufe what is attributed to the *Lord*, Exod. xxxii. 11. is in the 7th verfe of the fame chapter afcribed to *Mofes*: therefore *Mofes* is the *Lord*. And becaufe what is attributed to the Lord in *Ifaiah* lxv. 1. is in the xth of Romans, verfe 20. afcribed to *Ifaiah*; therefore *Ifaiah* is the *Lord*. And becaufe what is attributed to GOD, 2 Tim. i. 8, 9. is by *Paul* attributed to himfelf, 1 Cor. ix. 22. and to

---

* Twelve Arguments, in 12mo. 1647. p. 19, 20. or, Unitarian Tracts, v. i. p. 9.

Timothy,

Timothy, 1 Tim. iv. 16. therefore *Paul*, yea, *Timothy*, is GOD ‡.

These remarks are capable of an extensive application in the difpute concerning the effence of Chrift, and his equality with the Father. The laft obfervation in particular, affects almoft the whole feries of arguments in vindication of that opinion.

The tract, of which we are now fpeaking, though originally drawn up for the perufal of his friends, and for private ufe, was followed with the moft ferious confequences to the author, and with a great revolution in his condition.

‡ As before, p. 26, 27. or, Unitarian Tracts, v. i. p. 12.

SECTION

SECTION IV.

Proceedings against Mr. Biddle.

THERE is no act of iniquity, to which falſe zeal hath not prompted men. It hath not only drawn the ſword, and kindled the fire, to reſtrain and puniſh what has been deemed heretical pravity, but, when open and obvious proofs of it have not lain againſt a perſon, by interrogatories and tortures, it hath extorted confeſſions on which to ground a conviction. It hath conſtrued ſuſpicions into proofs. It hath invited or diſpoſed men to violate the confidence of friendſhip, and given a ſanction to perfidy. Of this the hiſtory of Mr. *Biddle* furniſhes a melancholy proof.

The *Twelve Arguments*, noticed in the laſt ſection, were communicated among others, to one, who, while Mr. *Biddle* moſt probably thought him a ſincere enquirer after truth, ſhewed himſelf unworthy

of

of any confidence. For, inftead of weighing the force of the reafoning, or endeavouring in the intercourfes of private friendfhip, to convince Mr. *Biddle* of its fallacy, he was ungenerous enough to betray him to the magiftrates of Gloucefter, and to the committee of the parliament, that then refided there.

The confequence of this information being lodged againft him was, that he was committed to the common goal, *December* 2, 1645. This commitment was cruel and peculiarly afflictive to him: for he was, at the time, ill of a dangerous fever. The defign of his imprifonment was to fecure his perfon, till the parliament fhould take cognizance of the affair. The feverity of this proceeding, happily, was foon mitigated by the interpofition of a compaffionate friend, a perfon of eminence in *Gloucefter*, who procured his enlargement, by giving bail for his appearance, when the parliament fhould fee fit to call him to their bar.

About

About *June*, 1646, Archbifhop *Ufher*, paffing through *Gloucefter*, in his way to *London*, had a conference with Mr. *Biddle*, refpecting his fentiments concerning the Trinity, and endeavoured to convince him that he was in an error, but without effect.

Six months after he was fet at liberty, Mr. *Biddle* was fummoned to appear at *Weftminfter*, and the parliament immediately chofe a committee, to whom the cognizance of his caufe was referred. Upon his examination, he freely and candidly confeffed, " that he did deny the commonly received opinion concerning the Deity of the Holy Ghoft, as he was accufed; but that he was ready to hear what could be oppofed to him, and if he could not make out his opinion to be true, honeftly to acknowledge his error.

He was urged to declare his fentiments concerning the Deity of *Chrift*, but he prudently waved the queftion, as not being to the point on which he was accufed, and as it was a fubject which he had not fufficiently

ciently ftudied, publickly to engage himfelf
on it.

Though he endeavoured to have his
affair brought to a conclufion on the fingle
queftion, which alone was properly before
his judges, no decifion was paffed; but he
was wearied out by tedious and expenfive de-
lays. This induced him, at the diftance of
fixteen months from his firft commitment,
to addrefs one of the committee, Sir *Henry
Vane*, in a letter dated *April* 1, 1647, in
which he folicits and befeeches that gentleman, if he had any bowels towards the
diftreffed, either to procure his difcharge, or
at leaft to make a report to the houfe,
touching his denial of the fuppofed Deity
of the Holy Spirit.

In this letter he plainly and fully expreffed his ideas concerning the nature and
offices of the Holy Spirit. " As for my
opinion touching the Holy Spirit, it is
that I believe the Holy Spirit to be the
chief of all miniftering fpirits, peculiarly
fent out from Heaven to minifter on their
behalf that fhall inherit falvation; and I do
place

place him, both according to the scriptures and the primitive Christians, and by name *Justin Martyr*, in his apology, in the third rank after God and Christ, giving him a pre-heminence above all the rest of the Heavenly Host. So that as there is one principal spirit amongst the evil angels, known in scripture by the name of *Satan*, or the *Adversary* *, or the *unclean* † *Spirit*, or the *evil Spirit of God* ‡, or the *Spirit of God* ‡, or the *Spirit* ‡ by way of eminence; even so there is one *principal Spirit* (I borrow this appellation from the Septuagint, who render the last clause of the 12th verse of Pfalm li. in this manner, πνευματι ηγεμονικω στηριξον με, *spiritu principali fulci me*; *stablish* me with thy principal spirit) there is, I say, one principal spirit amongst the good angels, called by the name of the *Advocate*, or the *Holy Spirit*, or the

---

* 1 Pet. 5. 8.　　† Zech. 13. 2.

‡ In support of the application of these terms to *Satan*, Mr. B. refers to 1 Sam. xvi. 15, 16, and last verse, and 1 Kings, xxii. 21. See the original.

Spirit *,

Spirit *, by way of eminence. This opinion of mine is attefted by the whole tenour of the fcripture, which perpetually
fpeaketh of him as differing from God, and
inferior to him †."

Then after an enumeration of many
texts which, in his apprehenfion, decidedly
fupported his fentiments, he adds fome
pertinent reflections on the importance of
the queftion, and the nature of the proceedings againft him.

" Behold now," fays he, " the caufe for
which I have lien under perfecution, raifed
againft me by my adverfaries, who being
unable to juftify by argument their practice of giving glory to the Holy Spirit, as
God, in the end of their prayers, fince there
is neither precept nor example for it in all
the fcripture, and being taxed by me for
giving the glory of God to another, and

---

* John xvi. 7. Ephef. iv. 30. Neh. ix. 20. 1
Cor. vii. 40. Acts x. 19.

† *Twelve Arguments.* Letter to a Member of
Parliament, p. or Unitarian Tracts, Vol. 1. p. 12.

worfhipping

worſhipping what he hath not commanded,
nor ever came into his heart, have in a
cruel and unchriſtian manner, reſorted to
the arm of fleſh, and inſtigated the ma-
giſtrate againſt me, hoping by his ſword
(not that of the ſpirit) to uphold their will-
worſhip; but in vain, ſince every plant
that the Heavenly Father hath not ſet ſhall
be rooted up. And that the practice of worſhipping the Holy Spirit of God, as God,
is ſuch a plant as God never ſet in his
word, would ſoon appear to the honourable
houſe, could they be ſo far prevailed with,
as having laid aſide all prejudice, ſeriouſly
to weigh the many and ſolid proofs that I
produce for my opinion out of the ſcripture, together with the ſlight, or rather
no proofs of the adverſe party for their
opinion; which they themſelves know not
what to make of, but that they endeavour
to delude both themſelves and others with
perſonalities, modes, ſubſtances, and ſuch
like brain-ſick notions, that have neither
ſap nor ſenſe in them, and were firſt hatched
by the ſubtilty of Satan in the heads of

C 6 *Platoniſts,*

Platonifts, to pervert the worfhip of the true God.

" Neither could this controverfy be fet on foot in a fitter juncture of time than this, wherein the Parliament and the Kingdom have folemnly engaged themfelves to reform religion both in difcipline and doctrine. For amongft all the corruptions in doctrine, which certainly are many, there is none that more deferveth to be amended than this, that fo palpably thwarteth the whole tenour of the fcripture, and trencheth to the very object of our worfhip, and therefore ought not to be lightly paffed over by a man that profeffeth himfelf a Chriftian, much more a Reformer. God is jealous of his honour, and will not give it to another; we therefore, as beloved children, fhould imitate our Heavenly Father therein, and not upon any pretence whatfoever depart from his exprefs command, and give the worfhip of the Supreme Lord of Heaven and Earth to him whom the fcripture no where affirmeth to be God.

" For

" For my own particular, after a long
impartial inquiry of the truth, in this controverſy, and after much and earneſt calling
upon God, to give unto me the ſpirit of
wiſdom and revelation in the knowledge of
him ; I find myſelf obliged, both by the
principles of reaſon and ſcripture, to embrace the opinion I now hold forth, and
as much as in me lyeth, to endeavour that
the honour of Almighty God be not transferred to another, not only to the offence
of God himſelf, but alſo of his Holy Spirit,
who can not but be grieved to have that
ignorantly aſcribed to himſelf, which is
proper to God that ſends him, and which
he no where challengeth to himſelf in ſcripture.

" What ſhall befall me in the purſuance
of this work, I refer to the diſpoſal of
Almighty God, whoſe glory is dearer to
me, not only than my liberty, but than my
life. It will be your part, Honored Sir,
into whoſe hands God hath put ſuch an
opportunity, to examine the buſineſs impartially, and to be an helper to the truth,
conſidering

confidering that this controverfy is of the greateft importance in the world, and that the divine truth fuffers herfelf not to be defpifed fcot-free.

"Neither let the meannefs of my outward prefence deter you from ftirring, fince it is the part of a wife man, as in all things, fo efpecially in matters of religion, not to regard fo much who it is that fpeaketh, as what it is that is fpoken; remembering how our Saviour in the Gofpel faith, that God is wont to hide his fecrets from the wife and prudent, and to reveal them unto children. In which number I willingly reckon myfelf, being confcious of my own perfonal weaknefs, but well affured of the evidence and ftrength of the fcripture to bear me out in this caufe *."

The effect of this pious and humble remonftrance was, that Sir *Henry Vane,* to whom it was addreffed, fhewed himfelf a friend to Mr. *Biddle,* and reported his cafe

---

* Twelve Arguments. The Letter written to a certain Knight, p. 6, 7, 8. or Unitarian Tracts, v. 1. p. 14, 15, 16.

to the houfe. The refult was not favourable to Mr. *Biddle*'s comfort and liberty, for he was committed to the cuftody of one of the officers of the Houfe of Commons, and he was continued under this reftraint for the five following years. In the mean time the matter was referred to the confideration of the Affembly of Divines, then fitting at *Weftminfter*, before fome of whom he often appeared, and gave them, in writing, his twelve arguments againft the Deity of the Holy Spirit.

The anfwer to his arguments, which he received at any of thefe interviews was not fatisfactory or convincing to his mind. This induced him to print them in the year 1647, in hopes that the publication of them would not only give the world a fair ftate of his cafe, but excite attention to the queftion. It was accompanied with an addrefs to the impartial reader, figned *J. H.* in which the writer expreffed his own and the author's earneft hope, that the publication of thefe arguments would engage fome one to attempt a folid reply to them; fuch a reply,

a reply, as would not merely tax his arguments with being weak and invalid, but,
by clear and ſtrong reaſonings, would refute
them, and carry conviction to inquiſitive
and doubting minds. A reply that did
not ſubſtitute railing for argument, and
ſupply the deficiency of its proofs by the bit-
terneſs of its invectives. " At theſe rates,"
he obſerved, " the weakeſt man might
eaſily ſubvert the ſtrongeſt controverſy."

This preface alſo beſpoke and in-
treated the reader's very ſerious attention
to the arguments laid before him ; " as to
a matter which affected the divine glory,
and his own ſalvation;" the author re-
queſted him, " at any hand to forbear
condemning his opinion as erroneous, till
he was able to bring pertinent and ſolid
anſwers to all his arguments."

To ſuppreſs the piece, and to prohibit
the progreſs of enquiry, it was juſtly obſerved, could " no ways unſcruple doubting ſpirits :" amongſt whom for the preſent
the writer numbered himſelf, expecting an
anſwer to theſe enſuing arguments, adding,

in

in the language of a pious and ingenuous
mind ; and that " God will be with him
that undertaketh it, and write in a fpirit of
meeknefs, and of wifdom, in the revelation
and knowledge of truth, fhall be the matter
of his prayers, who defires the truth may
be cleared up, and fhine like the noon-day,
and all error confounded, and vanifh before truth, like a mift before the fun."
J. H. *

The publication of this tract raifed a
great alarm, and it was called in and burnt
by the common hangman. But this illiberal mode of fuppreffing the work, and
ftifling enquiry, had only a fhort and
temporary effect. This piece, with two
other tracts, was reprinted by the author
in 1653, and it was publifhed a third time,
amongft the *Unitarian Tracts* in 4to, in the
year 1691. To which the life of the author was prefixed.

* Twelve Arguments, in 12mo. 1647.

SECTION

SECTION V.

Mr. *Biddle* publishes his *Confession of Faith*, and *Testimonies of the Fathers*.

MR. *Biddle* appears to have possessed a firmness of mind, which not only supported him under the dark clouds that gathered round him, but enabled him to pursue his enquiries, and to publish, with steadiness and freedom, his sentiments concerning the points for which he suffered. For, being yet in prison, he printed, in 1648, a *Confession of Faith concerning* the HOLY TRINITY, according to the scripture, with the *Testimonies of several of the Fathers on this head.*

In the conclusion of the preface to the *Confession of Faith*, he frankly expresses himself on the design of this publication, and the importance of its object. " I have," says he, " here presented you with a *Confession of Faith* touching the HOLY TRI-

NITY,

NITY, exactly drawn out of the fcriptures, with the texts alledged at large, that fo you may the better judge how fuitable the fame is to the word of God.

" Neither have I other aim in the publication thereof than to reftore that pure and genuine knowledge of God delivered in the fcripture, and which hath for many hundred years been hidden from the eyes of men, by the corrupt gloffes and traditions of Antichrift; who hath inftead thereof obtruded upon them I know not what abfurd and uncouth notions, bearing them in hand that ignorance is the mother of devotion, and that they then think and fpeak beft of God, when their conceits and words are moft irrational and fenfelefs. By which means having renounced thofe quiddities and ftrange terms, that have vitiated the fimplicity of the fcripture, and having laid afleep the contentations arifing from them, we fhall at length unanimoufly with one mouth glorify the God and Father of our Lord Jefus Chrift *."

* See the *Confeffion of Faith*, 12mo. 1648, or Unitarian Tracts, 4to. v. 1. Tract ii. 1691.

The

The preface, which clofes with the preceding paragraphs, is occupied with a full
reprefentation of the evils, of which Mr.
Biddle conceived the doctrine of the Trinity
had been productive, having, as he expreffeth
it, " not only made way for the idolatrous
pollutions of the Roman Antichrift, but,
lying at the bottom, corrupteth almoft our
whole religion."

To illuftrate and confirm this affertion,
he obferves that the common opinion touching three Perfons in God, fubverteth the
unity of God, fo frequently inculcated in
the fcripture; and that it hindereth men
from praying according to the prefcript of
the Gofpel, which inftructs us to afk of
God the Holy Spirit, and to pray to him
through his Son Jefus Chrift, which implieth that God is the Father only.

He alfo confiders the tenet of three Perfons in God as incompatible with the love
and honour which we owe to the moft High
God; this is the *higheft* love and honour
that it is in our power to exercife, and of
which *one perfon only* can be the object,
who

who can be the *Father only*, for the Son
and Spirit, as the names import, deriving
from him, can be only fecondary objects
of honour and love; in fubordination to
the Father, and with reference to the powers
and characters received from him.

He reprefents it as another confequence
of the common opinion, that it thwarteth
the idea, which men naturally entertain of
God, as the Being who is the firft caufe
of all things, exifting of himfelf only, and
all others from him. It looks therefore
like an attempt to deprive men of their
underftanding, and in a point of the greateft
importance, to afcribe Supreme Deity, to
two other perfons befides the Father, i. e.
to afcribe the character of the firft caufe,
of felf-exiftence, to beings who are caufed;
or, according to the orthodox ftyle, to the
Son, who is begotten of the Father, and to
the Holy Spirit, which proceedeth from
both.

Another confequence of this doctrine,
he alfo remarks, is, that it is a ftumbling
block to the antient people of God, the
Jews,

Jews, and is a bar to their reception of Chriftianity. "For they, having formerly fmarted for their idolatry, are now grown exceeding cautious of a tenet looking that way." He concludes with remonftrating on the effect which the doctrine of the Trinity has, in impeding the accomplifh-ment of the prophecy long fince delivered by *Zechariah*, ch. 14. 9. "In that day the LORD fhall be one, and his NAME ONE." Whereas, the partifans of this doc-trine contend, that the LORD is three, calling him *Deum Trinum*, and that his *Name* is not *One*, but three; even the Father, the Son, and the Holy Ghoft.

Having thus freely arraigned the com-mon doctrine of the Trinity, the author, in the following treatife, ftates and endea-vours to eftablifh his own ideas on the fubject. This he does under the form of fix articles or propofitions, each of which is feparately illuftrated by a full difcuffion of the principles it exhibits, and by a copious difplay of reafonings and divine authorities in proof of its truth.

A

A felection of the three firſt articles
may be entertaining and inſtructive, as well
as furniſh a ſpecimen of this performance.

I. " I believe that there is one moſt
high God, Creator of heaven and earth,
and firſt cauſe of all things pertaining to
our ſalvation, and conſequently the ulti-
mate object of our faith and worſhip ; and
that this God is none but the Father of
our Lord Jeſus Chriſt, the firſt perſon of
the Holy Trinity.

II. " I believe that there is one chief
Son of the moſt high God, or ſpiritual,
heavenly, and perpetual Lord and King,
ſet over the church by God, and ſecond
cauſe of all things pertaining to our ſalvation,
and conſequently the intermediate object of
our faith and worſhip ; and that this Son of
the moſt high God is none but *Jeſus Chriſt*,
the ſecond perſon of the Holy Trinity *.

III. " I believe that *Jeſus Chriſt*, to the
intent he might be our brother, and have
a fellow-feeling of our infirmities, and ſo
become the more ready to help us (the

* See p. 51. on the uſe of this word Trinity.

conſideration

confideration whereof is the greateft encouragement to piety that can be imagined)
hath no other than a human nature, and
therefore in this very nature is not only a
perfon, (fince none but an human perfon
can be our brother) but alfo our Lord,
yea, our God."

Were we to lay before the reader the
illuftrations and proofs brought forward,
under every article, we muft re-publifh
the tract at full length; yet it may be acceptable to point out fome remarks which
are recommended to our attention by their
novelty, or importance, or force.

Under the firft article he confiders the
text, Gen. 1. 26. *Let us make man*, as addreffed to the Holy Spirit, whom he con-
ceives to be reprefented in verfe 2. Pf. 104.
30. and Job 26. 13. as the inftrument of
God in the creation; upon which he ftarts
this queftion: " Had the Son of God,
Chrift Jefus, been alfo employed in creating
Adam, would he not likewife have been
mentioned in the hiftory of the creation?
Was it not as material, and altogether as

of

of great confequence for *Mofes* and the Jews to have known, that the Son of God *Chriſt Jeſus* was employed by God, in creating *Adam* as the Holy Spirit."

He grants that the holy fcripture attributeth Creation to *Chriſt*; but then he remarks, that by the nature of the thing itſelf, by the circumſtances of the places, and by exprefs words, it appears that not the firſt but fecond Creation, or the reduction of things into a new ſtate or order, is meant.

He argues, that *Chriſt* exprefsly precludes our conceiving of him as the Creator of Adam, when he afcribes it to another Being, Matt. 19. 14. in that defcription, HE *that made them.* He confiders this notion as totally incompatible with the language of *Peter* and *Paul* concerning *Chriſt*: the former fpeaking of him as *fore-ordained* or *fore-known* before the foundation of the world; which can be faid only of things that are to come, and are not already in being. The latter, Rom. 5. 14. defcribing *Adam as the Type of Him that was to*

come,

come, or as the Greek, *was to be*, μελλοῖης. Could *Adam* be a type of a being already exifting? or was the Creator of Adam yet to be; as yet to exift? or can it be faid of any one, that *he is to be*, when he is already in being?

Under the fecond article, he argues that Phil. 2. 5. can not be underftood to fpeak of what is called the Incarnation; becaufe the Apoftle, exhorting the *Philippians* to humility, from the example of *Chrift*, muft be fuppofed to draw his argument from fome inftance, that was confpicuous, and had been vifible to fight and contemplation, which the incarnation could not be. He further urges, that, in this paffage, the Apoftle fpeaks of our Lord only as a man.

On 1 Cor. 8. 6. *By whom are all things*, he remarks, by *all things* are not here meant all things fimply, but all things pertaining to our falvation, as is evident from this, that the Apoftle fpeaketh of Chriftians, and putteth an article before the word *all* in the Greek, which implieth reftriction *.

* δι ᾳ τα παῆα.

In

In difcuffing the third article concerning the ftrict humanity of Chrift, having quoted 2 Tim. 2. 5. John 3. 13. ch. 6. 62. ch. 8. 42. ch. 3. 14, 15. Matt. 9. 6, 7, 8. Matt. 16. 27, 28. Dan. 7. 13, 14. he obferveth, " that the moft excellent things which are in the fcripture attributed to *Chrift*, are attributed to him not only under the notion, but alfo under the very name of a *Man*."

In the title of the Tract, which we are reviewing ftands the word *Trinity,* and it frequently occurs in the following pages, as a term adopted by the author to convey a fcriptural truth. This, confidering the main drift and tendency of the Treatife, may furprize the reader. It may, certainly, be concluded from hence, that he had no objection to the ufe of the word; whether it was done with a defign more eafily to infinuate his ideas of the fcripture doctrine on this point, viz. that it confifted of *one God, one Lord,* and *one Spirit*; or whether it proceedeth from the mere force of early habit, which often laft of all permits us to

give

give up words, though we may long before have difcarded the ideas generally affixed to them.

But it is not duly confidered that the ufe of words, to which cuftom has long affixed a peculiar fenfe, will continue to awaken in the mind thofe ideas which they have generally been employed to exprefs; and that the force of the old meaning will prevail over any glofs or interpretation, with which we may accompany them. Would we get rid of error, we muft lay afide the *terms* under which it has been clothed, as well as explode the ideas themfelves. At leaft this fhould be done with refpect to fuch terms as, like the word Trinity, have no fanction from the language of fcripture, but are furely human inventions.

Mr. *Biddle*'s Confeffion of Faith was foon fucceeded by another Tract, entitled, The Testimonies of *Irenæus, Juftin Martyr, Novatianus, Theophilus* (who lived the two firft centuries after Chrift was born, or thereabouts) as alfo *Arnobius, Lactantius, Eufebius, Hilary,* and *Brightman*; concerning

cerning that one God and the perfons of
Holy Trinity. Together with obfervations on the fame, printed at London.

It may appear inconfiftent with the
avowed principles of Mr. *Biddle*, who pro-
feffed to derive his fentiments folely from
the fcriptures, that he fhould make an appeal to human teftimonies. The reafon
and propriety of his adopting this mode
of arguing are ftated by himfelf at the clofe
of this piece.

" Thofe human teftimonies above written have I alledged, not that I much regard them as to myfelf (who make ufe of
no other *rule* to determine controverfies
about religion, than the *fcripture*; and of
no other authentic *interpreter*, if a fcruple
arife concerning the fenfe of fcripture, than
reafon) but for the fake of the adverfaries,
who continually crake *the Fathers, the
Fathers*. And though fuch of them as
diffent from the Church of Rome, lay afide
this plea, when they have to do with Papifts about fundry points of controverfy;
yet do they take it up again, in a manner

waving

waving the scripture, when they argue with me.

" For it is apparent, that the Fathers of the two first centuries, or thereabouts, when the judgments of Christians were yet free, and not enslaved with the determinations of Councils, asserted the Father only to be that one God, and so were in the main right as to the faith concerning the HOLY TRINITY, however they went awry in imagining two natures in *Christ*, which came to pass (as we before hinted) partly because they were great admirers of *Plato*, and accordingly (as *Justus Lipsius* somewhere saith) did in *outward profession so put on Christ*, as that in heart they did *not put off Plato*, wittily applying his high notions touching the creation of the world, to what was simply and plainly spoken of the man *Christ Jesus*, in relation to the Gospel by the Apostle *John*; partly that they might thereby avoid the scandal of worshipping a *crucified man*, a thing then very odious amongst Jews and Pagans,

gans, and now amongſt deluded Chriſtians *."

Amongſt other paſſages cited by Mr. *Biddle* from the antient Chriſtian writers, is that from *Juſtin Martyr*, lately quoted by Dr. Prieſtley, whoſe inferences from it have been controverted by his opponents. It may therefore be acceptable to the reader, if we lay before him Mr. *Biddle*'s tranſlation of the paſſage, and remarks on it.

" *Nevertheleſs,* O Tryphon, *ſaid I, this remaineth ſafe, that ſuch a one is the Chriſt of God, although I can not demonſtrate that he was, before, the Son of the maker of all things, being a God, and was born a man by the Virgin, it being every way demonſtrated that he is the Chriſt of God, whoſoever otherwiſe he ſhall be found to be. But if I ſhall not demonſtrate that he did*

---

* The Teſtimonies, &c. printed in 12mo. p. 83, 84. or Unitarian Tracts, 4to. V. 1. Tract 4. p. 30.

pre-exiſt,

pre-exist, and according to the counsel of the Father, endured to be born a man of like affections with us, being endued with flesh, it is just and fit to say that I am mistaken in this only, and not to deny that he is the Christ, if he appear to be a man born of men, and to become the Christ by election.

" For there are some, dear friends, said I, of our kind, who confess him to be the Christ, yet hold him to be a man born of men. To whom I assent not; no, though very many of the same opinion with me should speak it, since we are commanded by Christ himself not to hearken to the doctrines of men, but to such things as have been promulgated by the Prophets of happy memory, and taught by himself.

" And TRYPHON replied, They that say he was a man, and according to election anointed and made Christ, methinks speak more probably, than you who say such things as you relate. For all we expect that the Christ shall be a man of men."

On

On this paſſage Mr. *Biddle* offers ſome
ſtrictures. " Obſerve here," Chriſtian
Reader, " that *Juſtin Martyr* did not think
it inconſiſtent that Jeſus ſhould be the
Chriſt, although he had no other than
the humane nature. Secondly, that divers
Chriſtians, whom *Juſtin* himſelf owned for
ſuch, for he ſaith that they were of the
ſame kind, and opinion with him, did then
de facto affirm that Jeſus, whom they
counted the Chriſt, had none but a humane nature. Both which were in the
ſucceeding age by *Athanaſius*, and ſince
by other ſuch like furious Zealots, ſtiffly
denied, and he pronounced utterly incapa-
ble of eternal life, who ſhould not believe,
not only that Chriſt had another nature,
but (what neither *Juſtin Martyr*, nor
any other of the Chriſtians, who lived in
the two firſt centuries, and whoſe works
are extant, ever did affirm) that that
other nature was the very nature of the
Moſt High God. Thirdly, that the Jews
(who would be happy, were their opi-

nion,

nion, concerning the kingdom of Chrift, as true as that they hold concerning his nature,) did not believe that the Chrift, who was to come, fhould be other than a man *."

* Teftimonies, p. 24, &c. ed. in 12mo. or, Unitarian Tracts, v. i. Tract 4. p. 9, 10. 18.

SECTION

SECTION VI.

A cruel Ordinance obtained against Mr.
Biddle.

IT is not fuppofeable that thefe pieces
of Mr. *Biddle* could be publifhed without drawing a great odium on their author,
or that this attack, on prevailing and eftablifhed opinions, could be made without
raifing indignation againft him. At that
time the fupreme power was folely in the
hands of the Parliament, the Epifcopalian
Hierarchy had been overturned, and in the
room of it had fucceeded a Prefbyterian
and Ecclefiaftical Government, the high
Court of which fat at *Wefminfter*, and
confifted of an Affembly of Divines. Thefe
took the alarm at the appearance of Mr.
Biddle's writings ; and, inftead of applying themfelves to the refutation of his fentiments by a candid and folid anfwer to his

arguments,

arguments, they applied to the civil power, and fupplied the defect of their own exertions by recourfe to its commanding terrors. They preferred the carnal to the fpiritual weapon, and found a more expeditious and popular remedy againft the rife of Herefy, in the ufe of the fword, than in that of the pen.

They accordingly folicited the interference of the Parliament, and prevailed with it to pafs an Ordinance for the punifhing of blafphemies and herefies; from which Mr. Biddle's life was in great danger; for though it took a wide compafs, and was formed to reach a variety of opinions, yet it was evidently pointed, in particular, againft the notions which he had advanced.

This Ordinance was directly pointed againft fuch as, in any mode, fhould not only deny the being, omniprefence, foreknowledge, almighty power, holinefs and eternity of God; but who fhould, by preaching, printing or writing, controvert the Deity of the Son, or of the Holy Spirit,

or

or the equality of Chrift with the Father, or the diftinction of two natures, the God-head and humanity, or the finlefs perfec-tion of his humanity, the meritorioufnefs of his death in behalf of believers; or that any of the books, commonly deemed cano-nical, were not the word of God. It pro-nounced thofe, who offended in any of thofe inftances, guilty of felony, and doom-ed them, if convicted on confeffion, or on the oaths of two witneffes, before two juftices, to imprifonment without bail or mainprize, until the next gaol-delivery, when the witneffes were bound to give evidence, and the party were to be indicted for felonious publifhing and maintaining fuch error. It then enacted, that in cafe the indictment fhould be found, and the party on his trial fhould not abjure the fame error, and maintenance and defence of the fame, that he fhould fuffer *the pains* of DEATH, as in cafe of felony, without be-nefit of clergy.

It appointed the fame procefs, and de-creed the fame fentence againft thofe who
had

had been formerly indicted on the fame grounds, and after having abjured their error, fhould again publifh and maintain the fame.

If the fanction by which this Ordinance enforced other determinations, wore a milder afpect, what was wanting in the feverity of its fentence, was counterbalanced by the rigour with which it extended and multiplied its decifions. To maintain and publifh that all men fhould be faved; that man hath by nature free-will to turn to God; that the foul dieth or fleepeth after the body is dead; that revelations or workings of the fpirit are a rule of faith; that man is bound to believe no more than by his reafon he can comprehend; that the two Sacraments of Baptifm and the Lord's Supper, are not ordinances commanded by the word of God; that baptifing Infants is unlawful, or fuch Baptifm is void, and that fuch perfons ought to be baptifed again, and in purfuance thereof fhall baptife any perfon formerly baptifed; that the obfervation of the Lord's day, as it is enjoined

by

by the laws and ordinances of this realm is not according to, or is contrary to, the word of God; or that it is not lawful to join in public prayer or family prayer, or to teach children to pray; or that the Churches of England are no more churches, nor their ministers and ordinances true ministers and ordinances; or that the church government by Presbytery is unlawful, or antichristian; or that magistracy, or the power of the civil magistrate by law established in England is unlawful, or that all use of arms, though for the public defence, (and though the cause be never so just) is unlawful. To advance or maintain any of these opinions, incurred, by this ordinance, imprisonment till the party should find two sufficient sureties, before two justices of the peace, one of them to be of the quorum, that he would not publish or maintain the same error or errors any more *.

The

* See CROSBY's History of the ENGLISH BAPTISTS, vol. I. p. 199. 205. or BRITISH BIOGRAPHY,

The enumeration of the opinions condemned by this ordinance (fome of which are omitted in this review) is fo minute, and full and pointed, as plainly to fpeak this language : " Our principles form an unerring ftandard, and not any deviation from it, in one inftance, is or fhall be admitted." No decree of any Councils, no Bull of any Pope could be more dogmatical, or authoritative ; few, if any, have been more fanguinary.

Befides the feverity of the penalties, which it denounced, the mode of procefs which it appointed, was arbitrary and repugnant to the conftitution of this country, in particular, as well as oppofite to the

PHY, vol. 6. p. 82. 84. This Ordinance is alfo preferved in " A Collection of Acts and Ordinances " of general ufe, made in the Parliament begun " and held at Weftminfter, the 3d of November, " 1648, and fince unto the adjournment of the Parliament begun and holden the 17th of September, " 1656, being a continuation of that work from " the end of Pulton's Collection." By Henry Scobell, Efq. Clerk of the Parliament. , Folio. 1658.

general

general principles of equity and juftice: for it allowed neither the privilege of a jury, nor the liberty of an appeal. Such is the operation of religious bigotry.

The truth, indeed is, that bigotry, though never amiable or reafonable, is comparatively an harmlefs thing, when it exifts only in individuals who are not armed with the power of the fword, nor can act with an united and combined influence and authority. The alliance of the Church with the State, gives the fting to this intolerant and baneful temper; and it matters little, whether the leaders in the Church fupport the rank of Bifhops, or move only in the humble poft of Prefbyters.

Both Epifcopacy and Prefbyterianifm " adopt one grand error, productive of two great evils, which generate ten thoufand more, all nefarious. The great and fountain error is the confidering of *Confcience* as a fubject of human government. This notion produces two great evils. 1. LEGISLATION; now all human legiflation

is

is oppreffive to confcience, and it is imma-
terial where this power is lodged. It is
TYRANNY any where. 2. Enforcing laws
made by *Jefus* by penal fanctions. In
popery and epifcopacy both the legiflative
and executive power are lodged in the fame
perfon. Prefbyterianifm is exactly like
them, and only fwears the civil magiftrate
to do the worft part of the work. From
thefe two evils, making laws for confcience
and then executing them, or executing
laws made by *Jefus Chrift*, by coercive
meafures, proceed confufion and **every evil
work *.**"

The conduct of the *Prefbyterians*, during
the fhort period, when they were in alliance
with the fupreme powers of this country,
verifies the truth of thefe remarks. In reference to *their* meafures *Milton* had every
reafon to fay with fatirical poignancy,
" New Prefbyter is but Old Prieft wrote
large."

* ROBINSON's Plan of Lectures on the Principles
of Nonconformity. 5th ed. 1781. p. 39, 40.

For

For the Ordinance, now before us, was only one, out of feveral public acts, that breathed the fame intolerant, dogmatical fpirit; and had the fame baneful afpect on the enquiries of the candid, and on the rights of confcience.

The fact is, that the queftion concerning the rights of confcience, had not been brought into a difcuffion; or, at leaft, the enquiry was only in its infancy. The object of conteft, between the *Epifcopalians* and *Prefbyterians*, had been not to eftablifh and enlarge the general liberty; but to gain power to themfelves, and to give fecurity to their own profeffions and opinions, under an idea that their own Creed, their own mode of worfhip alone was fcriptural; and, when eftablifhed, was to be maintained and protected by all the efforts of authority.

In the courfe of the conteft, the *Prefbyterians*, for a few years, gained the fuperiority. All thofe meafures were then right, which before they felt to be unjuft and oppreffive; becaufe now they were ufed

· in

in the caufe of God and Truth. Power blinded and corrupted *them*, as it had done before the *Epifcopalians*. An Ecclefiaftical Hierarchy, in every nation, in every age, under all civil revolutions, has been inimical to truth, and a bar to reformation.

In *Scotland* the Prefbyterian Hierarchy is meliorated by its neighbourhood to this country, and its union with the *Epifcopalian* Hierarchy under the fame King. But in *Geneva*, and in *Holland*, where it reigns exempt from the influence and controul of a different and powerful body of men, it is by no means favourable to liberty and free enquiry. The feverity of the Placarts, in the latter of thefe countries, has been a bar to the tranflation of the *Memoirs of the Life and Writings* of Fauftus Socinus, into Dutch. No bookfeller there having the courage to appear as the publifher of it. At *Dort* the tranflation of Dr. *Prieft-ley's Hiftory of the Corruptions of Chriftia-nity* has been ftrictly prohibited. And it may,. on good information, be afferted, that the fermons of the eftablifhed Clergy

of

of *Holland* have, in general, little of any moral inftruction; but the ftrain of them is dogmatical and intolerant.

It is an honour to the *Englifh Proteftant Diffenters* of this day, and a ground of devout thankfulnefs, that *Prefbyterianifm* hath no exiftence amongft them. They who, very improperly, are called *Prefbyterians*, as confiftent Proteftants, and as genuine advocates for liberty, have no rivals, and but few equals *.

But it is time to drop this fubject, and to return to Mr. *Biddle*, to whom, it was expected that the Ordinance, which has led us into thefe reflexions, would have proved fatal. Had it been more confined in its direction, it could fcarcely have failed of being deftructive to him. But its force was directed to fo many objects, and fo various, that it would have involved, in the execution of its fentence, many whom not

---

* See to this effect, the animated and eloquent Difcourfes delivered before the friends of the New Academy at Manchefter, in 1786, p. 25, &c. of Mr. Harrifon's Sermon.

only

only policy taught, but neceſſity conſtrained them, to ſpare. For in the army, from which quarter the authority of Parliament met with conſiderable oppoſition, numbers, both of ſoldiers and officers, were liable to the ſeverities of this act. On this account, and becauſe there was a diſſenſion in the Parliament itſelf, it laid unregarded for ſeveral years.

SECTION

SECTION VII.

Mr. Biddle's Sufferings from **1648** *to* 1651. *His subsequent enlargement and improvement of* **it.**

THOUGH the circumstances noticed in the close of the last Section, enervated to a great degree, the force of that shocking Ordinance, which was aimed at Mr. *Biddle's* life, yet he suffered, for several years, the miseries of a severe imprisonment. It derived, however, some mitigation, and indeed, enlargement through the death of Charles **I.**

In the subsequent confusion of the times arising from the opposition that the Commonwealth met with from the Royalists, the Scots and the Irish, and from the conduct of the Presbyterians towards the New Government, the attention of the Parliament and of the Presbyterians was naturally

turally drawn off from religious difputes to
the eftablifhment of their power and influence in the political fcale. The Parliament alfo interfered with explicit and
direct exertions in favour of Toleration.

For *Cromwell*, before he embarked for
Ireland, which he was appointed to reduce,
fent letters to the Parliament, urging the
repeal of all the penal laws relating to
religion. His application was fupported
by a petition from General *Fairfax*, and
his Council of Officers, praying that all
penal ftatutes formerly made, whereby
many confcientious people were molefted,
might be removed. This petition was
favourably received, and after fome time
paffed into a law.

Though it does not appear that Mr.
Biddle, in confequence of this, was difmiffed from prifon by a legal and official
difcharge, yet, for the prefent, thefe
meafures were favourable to him. His
keeper allowed him more liberty, and permitted him, upon fecurity being given, even
to go into *Staffordfhire*. Here the obloquy
and

and confinement, which he had fuffered, were, in fome degree, foothed and counterbalanced by the patronage and kindnefs of a Juftice of the Peace, who received him into his houfe, courteoufly entertained him, made him his Chaplain, and appointed him to be Preacher of a Church in that county, and at his death left him a legacy; which was a very feafonable fupply to him, as he had already fpent nearly all his fubftance in about four years chargeable reftraint *. One regrets, that the Memoirs of Mr. *Biddle* have not perpetuated the name of the gentleman who acted this excellent part. He evidenced a laudable fuperiority to vulgar prejudices, in not being afhamed of this perfecuted man; and he manifefted a chriftian benevolence and fortitude, in affording to him his patronage, and in miniftring to his wants. It is a pleafing thought, that though the names of thofe who perform fuch good deeds, fhould be loft to the

* Britifh Biography, v. 6. p. 85.

E   world,

world, they are on everlasting record in the books of Heaven.

Mr. *Biddle* was not long permitted to enjoy the ease and comfort of his friendly asylum, for Sir *John Bradshaw*, President of the Council of State, being informed of his retreat, issued out orders for his being recalled, and more strictly confined. In this long confinement, which lasted to *February*, 1651, what proved most grievous to him, was that by reason of his lying under the imputation of blasphemy and heresy, the minds of people were, either so alienated from him, or so intimidated with an apprehension of incurring the same odium, should they shew him any kind and respectful attention, that he was cut off from all the intercourses of life, and could hardly have any one to converse with. In particular, no divine, except Mr. *Peter Gunning*, afterwards Bishop of *Ely*, during his seven years confinement, ever paid him a visit, not even to attempt to convince him of his errors. A good man, suffering for conscience and his love

of

of truth, muft be very fenfibly affected with a treatment, which expreffes not only neglect, but contempt and hatred.

A worthy fucceffor to Mr. *Biddle*, in the like fufferings, and for the fame caufe, the excellent Mr. *Emlyn*, felt the full force of this trial. " During this more than two whole years imprifonment," fays he, " my former acquaintance (how intimate foever before) were altogether eftranged from me, and all offices of civility in a manner ceafed; efpecially among them of fuperior rank, though a few of the plainer tradefmen of my own people were more compaffionate and kind. O! my God, what a change haft thou made in my 'outward condition! I had a tolerable efteem, and a multitude of friends, but am now become their fcorn and bye-word, and my acquaintance and friends ftand afar off *."

Thus bigotry cancels the bonds of life, and heretical pravity is looked on as more

* *Emlyn*'s Works, vol. 1. p. 36. 4th ed. 1746. Memoirs of his Life, p. 32.

criminal

criminal than the moft heinous acts of immorality. A robber and a murderer is treated according to the rights of humanity, and is indulged with the vifit of fympathy and friendfhip, which is denied to the man who deviates from the prevailing faith, though his character in every other refpect, is blamelefs and excellent; denied by thofe, who profefs a religion which inculcates *vifiting the Prifoner*, as an expreffion of refpect, of attachment and gratitude to its great author. But fo it pleafeth providence, that the cup of which the fufferer for righteoufnefs fake partaketh, fhould be mingled with every bitter ingredient, to try his faith, to exalt his virtue, and to fhew the power of truth, furmounting, in the end, every evil and difficulty.

In the experience of Mr. *Biddle,* poverty was added to imprifonment and the neglect of mankind. Notwithftanding the recruit which his fortune had received from the legacy juft mentioned, his fubftance, in the courfe of feven years confinement, was all fpent, and he was reduced to fuch indigence,

digence, that, unable to pay for the ordinary repaſt of the table, he was glad, ſays his Biographer, " of the cheaper ſupport of drinking a draught of milk from the cow, morning and evening."

When he was reduced to this ſituation, and had been ſo long precluded from all the means of ſupport, which the benevolence of others, or his own induſtry might ſupply, Divine Providence did not leave him to periſh through want, but opened for him an unexpected reſo rce. Mr. *Roger Daniel*, a Printer of *London*, formed at that time the deſign of publiſhing a new and moſt accurate edition of the Greek Verſion of the Old Teſtament, called the *Septuagint*. At the recommendation of a learned man, he employed Mr. *Biddle* to correct the impreſſion, knowing full well, ſays Mr. *Wood*, that *Biddle* was an exact Grecian, and had time enough to follow it. This was an employment not only ſeaſonable, but moſt acceptable to Mr. *Biddle*, " whoſe delight," obſerves the writer of his life, " was in the law of God.

E 3   This

This and another employment of a more private nature, did, for some time, furnish him with a comfortable subsistence *."

In the year 1651, such public measures were taken, as, by their operation were favourable to our virtuous sufferer; for the Parliament published an Act of Indemnity for all crimes, with a few exceptions; which did not reach the case of those who were confined for advancing and disseminating what were deemed heretical opinions. This act restored, among others, Mr. *Biddle* to full liberty.

In consequence of the pieces he had published, and of the severe proceedings against him, it appears, that an attention to the general question was awakened ; and some had been made converts to his principles, particularly in *London*. The liberty which he now obtained, was improved by his meeting, on every Lord's day, with those friends he had gained in the city, for the purpose of expounding the scriptures, and discoursing thereon.

* Wood's *Athenæ Oxonienses*. Art. *Biddle*.

The

The principle, on which Mr. *Biddle* and his adherents, firſt formed themſelves into a diſtinct and ſeparate ſociety was, that the *Unity of God is an Unity of Perſon as well as Nature*; that the Holy Spirit is indeed a perſon, but not God. The object of their religious aſſociation was to exert their endeavours, that the honour of Almighty God ſhould not be transferred to another. For, as Mr. *Biddle* urges, in a piece before quoted, " God is jealous of his honour, and will not give it to another; we therefore, as beloved children, ſhould imitate our Heavenly Father herein, and not upon any pretence whatſoever depart from his expreſs command, and give the worſhip of the Supreme Lord of heaven and earth to him whom the ſcripture no where affirmeth to be God."

Mr. *Biddle*'s ſociety, emancipated from the reſtraints of an eſtabliſhment, and aſſembling together, not only for the purpoſe of divine worſhip, but, for freely inveſtigating theological queſtions, adopted ſome

other

other difcriminating notions.   Such as
thefe; " that the Fathers under the Old
Covenant had only temporal promifes;
that faving faith confifted in univerfal obedience performed to the commands of God
and Chrift; that Chrift rofe again only by
the power of his Father, not his own; that
juftifying faith is not the pure gift of God,
but may be acquired by mens' natural
abilities; that faith cannot believe any thing
contrary to, or above reafon; that there is
no *original Sin*; that *Chrift* hath not the
fame body now in glory, in which he fuffered and rofe again; that the faints fhall
not have the *fame* body in heaven which
they had on earth; that *Chrift* was not
Lord or *King* before his refurrection, or
Prieft before his afcenfion; that the faints
fhall not, before the day of judgment,
enjoy the blifs of heaven; that God doth
not certainly know future contingencies;
that there is not any authority of Fathers
or general Councils in determining matters
of faith; that *Chrift* before his death had

not

not any dominion over the Angels, and
that *Chrift* by dying made no fatisfaction
for us *."

The members of this fociety were called,
from Mr. *Biddle*, their head and paftor,
Bidellians; and from their agreement in
opinion, concerning the Unity of God and
the humanity of *Chrift*, with the followers
of *Socinus*, they were denominated *Socinians*. " They followed indeed, at firft,
Mr. *Biddle* (as he efpoufed the tenets of
Socinus) but fo, that as foon as there appeared better light, (to ufe a fcripture
phrafe) *they rejoiced in it*." The name, which
moft properly characterifed their leading
fentiment and detachment from an implicit
adherence to any teacher, was that of *Unitarians*.

This was the rife of the Englifh *Unitarians*, to whofe honour it was faid, that
" befides an acutenefs and dexterity of

---

* See the Preface to Sir PETER PETT's *Happy
Future State of England*, as quoted by *Mofheim's*
Tranflator. MOSHEIM's *Ecclefiaftical Hiftory*, vol. v.
p. 56. note *(rr)* of the 2d edition in 8vo. 1757.

thought, they were excellently learned, especially in sacred Criticism." But " that which most commended them, was the freedom and sincerity, which they all along practised, in judging of the controverted Articles of Religion."

It is justice to the worthy persons themselves, and useful to posterity and the cause of truth, to perpetuate, if possible, the names of those who have been its Patrons and Advocates, or Sufferers for it ; and who, by their exertions, though not by their pen, have contributed to the spread of religious knowledge and free enquiry. We regret it, that of those who were Mr. *Biddle*'s friends, and members of the church which he raised, only two names have been preserved to us, those of Mr. *Nathaniel Stuckey* and Mr. *Thomas Firmin.*

The first was a young gentleman, eminent for his distinguished parts and early piety. He was born in 1649. At the age of fifteen he published a Latin translation of Mr. *Biddle*'s Scripture Catechism,

for

for the ufe of Foreigners; and in the next
year 1665, he printed a Latin Verfion of
Mr. *Biddle's Brief Catechifm for Children*;
to which he annexed an Oration of his
own, in the fame language, on the fufferings and death of Chrift *. This young
man died at the age of feventeen †.

* **To** this edition of **Mr.** *Biddle*'s Catethetical
pieces was alfo fubjoined, a letter addreffed to him
by *Jeremiah Felbinger*, a zealous Unitarian, who
was born in *Silefia*, but having been obliged often
to change his refidence, on account of his fentiments, died in *Amfterdam*, where he fupported himfelf by the care of a School, and correcting the
prefs. The purport of the letter, juft mentioned,
was to exprefs his joy in the acquifition of fuch a
man to the party of the *Antitrinitarians*; and to
convey his earneft wifhes, fupported by various
arguments, that he would go on to exert himfelf
in the fame caufe, and would diffeminate the fentiments he adopted, **not** only in *England*, but in
the new world. Vide **Fr.** Sam. *Bock* Hiftoria
Antitrinitariorum, vol. 1. 8vo. 1776. *Art. Felbingerius*.

† Sandii *Bibliotheca Antitrinitariorum*. Art. **Bi-
dellius** & Felbingerius.

E 6   But

But the greateſt honour and ſupport were derived to Mr. *Biddle* and his cauſe from the friendſhip and exertions of Mr. *Thomas Firmin*, the friend and intimate of the Doctors *Outram, Whichcote* and *Worthington*, and of the Biſhops *Wilkins, Tillotſon* and *Fowler*; a man of eminent piety and ſuperior virtue; who, for active and generous benevolence, has had few equals in any age. Biſhop Burnet ſays of him, that " he was in great eſteem for promoting many charitable deſigns, for looking after the poor of the city, and ſetting them to work : for raiſing great ſums for ſchools and hoſpitals, and indeed for charities of all ſorts, private and public. He had ſuch credit with the richeſt Citizens, that he had the command of great wealth as often as there was occaſion for it *." His time was devoted to benevolent exertions; his fortune was laid out in liberal, munificent deeds. The Hoſpitals

---

* Bp. *Burnet's* Hiſtory of his own Times, v. 3. 8vo. p. 292.

of St. *Thomas* and of *Chrift* particularly
felt the influence, and continue to enjoy
the good effects, of his generofity and
activity. In the cloifter of the latter, a
marble records and perpetuates the praifes
of his wonderful zeal and charity †.

Mr. Firmin, befides being the perfonal
friend of Mr. *Biddle*, continued, after his
deceafe, and until after the revolution, with
much vigour and affiduity, to promote the
reception of his opinions. He encouraged
many publications in defence of the Unity
of God, which he difperfed over the nation, diftributing them freely to all who
would accept of them. He had a particular concern in the publication of feveral
volumes of *Unitarian* Tracts in 4to. which
iffued forth from the prefs about the time
of the Revolution.

Mr. *Firmin* was a very young man when
Mr. *Biddle*'s fociety was firft formed ; and
it does not appear, that it fubfifted after

† For a full account of his moft ufeful and generous deeds, fee his Life by Mr. *Cornifh*.

the

the death of its founder, who did not attempt to bring his friends into fuch clofe
bonds of union, as would preferve them
a diftinct community after his removal.
The force of the teftimony, which was
borne to the doctrine of the divine unity
by the writings of the *Unitarians* could not,
but be greatly diminifhed by the diffolution of Mr. *Biddle*'s Society. It is to
be lamented, that Mr. *Firmin*, in particular, did not exert himfelf to keep together this body of Unitarians, or that, if, as
one would hope, he did take fome fteps
with this defign, they were not fuccefs-
ful.

SECTION

SECTION VIII.

Mr. Biddle's Dispute with Dr. Gunning, and Publication of his Catechism.

WHILE Mr. *Biddle* and his friends enjoyed the liberty of holding religious assemblies, Dr. *Gunning*, afterwards *Regius Professor* of Divinity at *Cambridge*, and Bishop of *Ely*, who had visited Mr. *Biddle* in prison, and was eminent as a learned man, and as a ready, acute Disputant, came, on a Lord's day in the year 1654, to their meeting, accompanied with some learned friends. His conduct soon explained his intentions and views, that they were not to be an hearer of Mr. *Biddle*, and a witness of the order of his worship; but publicly and before his own adherents, to confound and confute him. For he commenced a disputation with him, on the first time, concerning the Deity of

the

the Holy Spirit; and then, on the next Lord's day, concerning the fupreme Deity of Chrift. The difputation was carried on in the fyllogiftic mode, and they took their turns of refponding and oppofing.

Mr. *Biddle* was evidently taken at a great difadvantage, as he was fuddenly furprifed into a debate without any defigned preparation for it. But this circumftance contributed to difplay both his furniture and abilities, and to fhew how much he had ftudied the queftions, and was mafter of the argument. For his Biographer informs us, that Mr. *Biddle* acquitted himfelf with fo much learning, judgment and knowledge in the fenfe of the Holy Scriptures, that inftead of lofing, he gained much credit both to himfelf and his caufe, as even fome of the gentlemen of Dr. *Gunning*'s party had the ingenuity to acknowledge *."

But the Doctor, unwilling to fet down as foiled, or prefuming on his own fupe-

---

* Unitarian Tracts. Biddle's Life, p. 6, 7.

riority

riority in another queftion ; after this, furprifed Mr. *Biddle* a third time ; and finding
him in the difcuffion of the argument
againft the fatisfaction of punitive juftice
by the death of *Chrift*, he defended that
fentiment with great vigour. But on this,
as on the former occafions, he met with
a fkilful and dexterous opponent ; which
he had the generofity, afterwards, to confefs.

This method of attack, by intruding,
unawares, upon a religious fociety, and
interrupting their worfhip, or by difcuffing
controverted points in a public difputation,
hath, very properly, been laid afide, and
given way, in our more liberal age, to
the ufe of the pen. There was a rudenefs
and violence in it, from which modern
politenefs is juftly averfe ; and it favoured
more of the fpirit of contention, and an
eagernefs for victory, than of the love of
truth. Yet public difputation was a mode
of oppofing fuppofed error, generally
practifed, through Europe, from the time
of

of the Reformation till the close of the last
century. What ever advantage might
arife from fuch public difcuffion of theological queftions, by awakening the attention of men, and exciting them to think
and enquire on fubjects, to which perhaps
they would not, otherwife, have turned
their thoughts; yet they were productive
of much evil, by inflaming the fpirits of
men. They thus tended to beget in fome
a diflike, and in others a contempt of
religious debate; while the prevailing party
took occafion to triumph with all the info-
lence of power.

But to return — this year of Mr. *Biddle's*
life was diftinguifhed more by the publication of two *Catethetical* pieces, than by
his public difputations with Dr. *Gunning*.
They were entitled, " A Two-fold Cate-
" chifm; the one fimply called *A Scrip-*
" *ture Catechifm* ; the other *A Brief Scrip-*
" *ture Catechifm* for Children; wherein
" the chiefeft points of the Chriftian Reli-
" gion, being queftion-wife propofed, re-
" folve themfelves by pertinent anfwers
" taken

" taken word for word out of the Scrip-
" ture, without either confequences or
" comments. Compofed for their fakes,
" that would fain be *mere Chriftians*, and
" not of this or that fect, inafmuch as all
" the fects of Chriftians, by what names
" foever diftinguifhed, have more or lefs
" departed from the fimplicity and truth
" of the fcripture." The difcriminating
title of the other runs, *A Brief Scripture
Catechifm for Children*; wherein, notwithftanding the brevity thereof, all things neceffary unto life and godlinefs are contained.
By *John Biddle*, Mafter of Arts, of the
Univerfity of *Oxford*.

In the preface to the firft of thefe, Mr.
Biddle complains, that all Catechifms were
generally fo filled with the fuppofitions and
traditions of men; that " the leaft part of
them was derived from the word of God."
For, fays he, " when Councils, Convoca-
tions and Affemblies of Divines, juftling
the facred writers out of their place in the
church, had once framed Articles and
Confeffions

Confeffions of Faith according to their own
fancies and interefts, and the Civil Magiftrate had by his authority ratified the
fame, all Catechifms were afterwards fitted
to thofe Articles and Confeffions, and the
Scripture either wholly omitted, or brought
in only for a fhew, not one quotation
amongft many being a whit to the purpofe,
as will appear to any man of judgment, who
taking into his hands the faid Catechifms,
fhall examine the texts alledged in them;
for if he do this diligently and impartially,
he will find the Scripture and thofe Catechifms to be " at fo wide a diftance from
one another, that he will begin to queftion,
whether the Catechifts gave any heed at
all to what they wrote, and did not only
themfelves refufe to make ufe of their reafon, but prefume that their readers alfo
would do the fame."

To prevent the evils of this method,
Mr. *Biddle* profeffes, that, according to
the underftanding he had obtained by con-
tinual meditation on the word of God, he
had compiled his Scripture Catechifm;

in which he himfelf afferted nothing, but only introduced the Scripture faithfully uttering its own affertions, which all Chriftians confefs to be of undoubted truth.

Mr. *Biddle*, aware that his Catechifm would exhibit fentiments contrary to the current opinions of the age, cautions his reader againft taking offence at them. " Take heed, that thou fall not foul upon them, for thou canft not do fo, without falling upon the holy Scripture itfelf, inafmuch as all the anfwers throughout the whole Catechifm are faithfully tranf-cribed out of it, and rightly applied to the queftions, as thou thyfelf mayeft perceive, if thou fhalt make a diligent infpection into the feveral texts with all their circum-ftances."

To the objection, that he was apprehen-five would be made to the defign for which fome texts were cited, viz. that they ought to be underftood figuratively: he protefts againft putting figurative interpre-
tations

tations on the Scripture, without exprefs
warrant of the Scripture itfelf; as a method
of interpretation fubject to no certain rule,
and which might be applied to the fupport
of any abfurdity. " Certainly might we
of our own heads, argues he, figuratively
interpret the fcripture; when the letter is
neither repugnant to our fenfes, nor to
the fcope of refpective texts, nor to a
greater number of plain texts to the contrary, (for in fuch cafes we muft of neceffity admit figures in the facred volume,
as well as we do in profane ones, otherwife
both they and it will clafh either with
themfelves, or with our fenfes, which the
fcripture itfelf intimates to be of infallible
certainty, fee 1 John 1, 2, 3.) might we,
I fay, at our pleafure, impofe our figures
and allegories on the plain words of God,
the fcripture would in very deed be, what
fome blafphemoufly affert it to be, a *nofe
of wax.*

His reflexions on the confufion of language introduced into the Chriftian Religion, by the invention of intricate and
unfcriptural

unfcriptural terms and phrafes, which are
not underftood, either by the people, or
by thofe that invented them, deferve attention. Wherefore, fays he, there is no
poffibility to reduce the Chriftian religion
to its primitive integrity, (a thing, he
obferves, never fincerely attempted, even
in the reformed Churches, fince men have,
by fevere penalties, been hindered from
proceeding further than did *Luther* or
Calvin) but by cafhiering thofe many intricate terms and devifed forms of fpeaking impofed on our religion, and **by** wholly
betaking ourfelves to the plainnefs of the
fcripture. For **I** have long fince obferved
(and find my obfervation to be true and
certain) that when to exprefs matters **of**
religion, men make ufe of words and phrafes
unheard of **in the** fcripture, **they** flily
under them couch falfe **doctrines, and ob-**
trude them **on us ; for** without queftion **the**
doctrines of the **fcripture** can be fo **aptly**
explained in no language, as that of fcrip-
ture itfelf."

After

After a full enumeration of various terms, introduced into Theology, Mr. Biddle remarks: " After *Conſtantine* the Great, together with the Council of *Nice*, had once deviated from the language of the Scripture in the buſineſs touching the Son of God, calling him co-eſſential with the Father; this opened a gap for others afterwards, under a pretence of guarding the truth from Heretics, to deviſe new terms at pleaſure, which did by degrees ſo vitiate the chaſtity and ſimplicity of our faith delivered in the Scripture, that there hardly remained ſo much as one point thereof ſound and entire. So that as it was wont to be diſputed in the ſchools, whether the old ſhip of *Theſeus* (which had in a manner been wholly altered at ſundry times, by the acceſſion of new pieces of timber upon the decay of the old) were the ſame ſhip it had been at firſt, and not rather another by degrees ſubſtituted in the ſtead thereof. In like manner, there was ſo much of the primitive truth worn

away

away by the corruption, that did by little and little overfpread the generality of Chriftians, and fo many errors inftead thereof tacked to our religion at feveral times, that one might juftly queftion, whether it were the fame religion with that which *Chrift* and his Apoftles taught, and not another fince devifed by men, and put in the room thereof.

But thanks be to God, through our Lord *Jefus Chrift*, who amidft the univerfal corruption of our religion, hath preferved his written word entire, (for had men corrupted it, they would have made it fpeak more favourably in behalf of their lufts and worldly interefts, than it doth) which word, if we with diligence and fincerity pry into, refolving to embrace the doctrine that is there plainly delivered, though all the world fhould fet itfelf againft us for fo doing, we fhall eafily difcern the truth, and fo be able to reduce our religion to its firft principles.

" For thus much I perceive by my own experience, who being otherwife of no

F

great

great abilities, yet fetting myfelf with the aforefaid refolution, for fundry years together, upon an impartial fearch of the Scripture, have not only detected many errors, but prefented the readers with a body of Religion, exactly tranfcribed out of the word of God; which body, whofoever fhall well ruminate and digeft in his mind, may by the fame method, wherein I have gone before him, make a further enquiry into the Oracles of God, and draw forth whatfoever yet lies hid, and being brought to light, will tend to the accomplifhment of godlinefs amongft us, for at this only all the Scripture aimeth: I fay the Scripture, which all men, who have thoroughly ftudied the fame, muft of neceffity be enamoured with, as breathing out the mere wifdom of God, and being the exacteft rule of a holy life (which all religions whatfoever confefs to be the way unto happinefs) that can be imagined, and whofe divinity will never, even to the world's end, be queftioned by any but fuch as are unwilling to deny

their

their wordly lufts, and obey the pure
and perfect precepts. Which obedience
whofoever fhall perform, he fhall not only
in the life to come, but even in this life,
be equal to the angels."

Mr. *Biddle's Scripture Catechifm*, which
is introduced by thefe reflexions, is divided into twenty-four chapters; com-
prifing a fyftem of fpeculative and prac-
tical Theology. The fubjects are, of
the Holy Scripture, or word of God; of
God; of the Creation; of Chrift *Jefus*;
of the *Holy Ghoft*; of Salvation by *Chrift*;
of *Chrift's* mediation; of *Chrift's* pro-
phetic office; of remiffion of fins by
Chrift; of *Chrift's* kingly office; of *Chrift's*
prieftly office; of *Chrift's* death; of the
univerfality of God's love; of *Chrift's* refurrection; of Juftification and Faith; of
keeping the commandments, and having
an eye to the reward; of perfection in
virtue and godlinefs to be attained, and
of departing from righteoufnefs and faith;
of the duty of Subjects and Magiftrates;
Wives and Hufbands, Children and Pa-

F 2   rents,

rents, Servants and Masters; of the behaviour of men and women in general,
and, in special, of aged men, aged women, young women and young men; of
Prayer; of the Church; of the Government and Discipline of the Church; of
Baptism; of the Lord's Supper; of the
Resurrection of the dead and the last judgement; and what shall be the final condition of the righteous and the wicked
thereupon.

This piece, though drawn up purely
in the words of Scripture, was formed with
a pointed reference to the opinions, which
he conceived had no foundation in the
Scriptures; and many of his quotations
were so constructed as to introduce the
texts which appeared, explicitly and plainly,
to stand in contrast with those sentiments.
For instance,

In the chapter of GOD, there is this
general question concerning the love of
the Divine Being: Could we love him
with *all the heart*, if he were *three?* Or

is

is his *Onenefs* the caufe hinted by *Mofes,* why we fhould love him thus? How found the words according to the truth of the Hebrew text? See *Ainfworth*'s tranfla- tion.

Anfwer.—" Hear, O Ifrael, the Lord our God, the Lord is ONE." Deut. vi. 4.

In the chapter on the Kingly Office of *Chrift,* there is another example of this pointed reference, viz. " Ought men to honour the Son as they honour the Fa- ther, becaufe he hath the *fame Effence* with the Father, or becaufe he hath the fame judiciary power? What is the deci- fion of the Son himfelf concerning this point? Anf. " The Father judgeth no man, but hath *committed all judgement* unto the Son; that *all men fhould honour the Son, even as they honour the Father.*" John v. 22, 23. 2. Did the Father give judiciary power to the Son becaufe he had in him the *divine nature perfonally united to the human*; or becaufe he was the *Son of Man?* What is the decifion of the Son concerning this point alfo? Anf.

F 3   " He

" He hath given him authority to exe-
cute judgement, becaufe *he is the Son of
Man.*"

On the head of Juftification we meet
alfo with fome queftions, clofe and pointed,
after the fame manner. E. g. 2. In the
Juftification of a believer is the righteoufnefs of Chrift imputed to him, or his own
faith for righteoufnefs? Anf. " To him
that worketh not, but believeth on him
that juftifieth the ungodly, *his faith is
counted for righteoufnefs.*" 2. Doth not
God juftify men, becaufe of the full price
that *Chrift* paid to him in their ftead, fo
that he abated nothing of his right, in
that one drop of *Chrift's* blood is fufficient to fatisfy for a thoufand worlds? If
not, how are they faved? Anf. " Being
juftified FREELY by his grace, through the
redemption, that is in *Chrift Jefus;* in
whom we have redemption through his
blood, the *forgivenefs of fin,* according to
the *riches of his grace,* Rom. 3. 24. Eph.
1. 7." ·

Should

Should it be thought that this mode of introducing and refuting the fentiments of others, has too much the air of controverfy, perfectly to fuit the defign of a Catechifm profeffedly fcriptural; it muft be allowed to be a pertinent and forcible way of bringing into view texts that feemed to be overlooked; and of fhewing that the language of the other party was totally unfcriptural, and their conclufions from fome particular paffages abfolutely repugnant to the plain declarations of other texts.

The Catechifm which we have reviewed, was too prolix for the attention and memory of Children; of this Mr. *Biddle* appears to have been fully fenfible; for as it has been noticed, he connected with it another catethetical compofition called " A Brief Catechifm for Children:" " Whether, he fays in the preface, in years or underftanding; that they might receive true and folid information concerning the chief articles of the Chriftian faith."

F 4 " Yea,"

" Yea," he adds, " perhaps it may
(as well as the larger Catechifm going
before) give further light and inftruction
even to them, who feem to have attained
a full ftature in the knowledge of the
Gofpel. For, though all the things, whether of belief or practice that are either
neceffary or very profitable to the attainment of eternal life, be plainly delivered
in the Scripture, yet confidering in what
principles Chriftians are generally edu-
cated, it would perhaps have been impoffible for them, having the eyes of their
underftanding fo veiled with prejudicate
opinions, to fee what is clearly held forth
in the Scripture, and accordingly with
eafe fetched out from hence by me, who
have long fince difcarded prejudices, and
am (through the fpecial favour of *Jefus
Chrift* towards me) addicted to none of
thofe many factions in Religion, where-
into the Chriftian world hath, to its infinite hurt, been divided, but rejoice to be
a *mere Chriftian,* admitting (as I have
elfewhere

elſewhere declared) no other rule of faith
than the Holy Scripture, (which all Chriſtians, though otherwiſe at infinite va-
riance amongſt themſelves in their opinions
about Religion, unanimouſly acknowledge
to be the word of God) nor any other interpreter, if a doubt ariſe about the meaning of the Scripture, than reaſon; which
all ſober men confeſs to be the only principle that God hath implanted in us to
judge between right and wrong, good and
bad, and whereby we excel all other living
creatures whatſoever."

" The Lord Jeſus grant, that this and
the foregoing larger Catechiſm may by
the Readers be peruſed as profitably, as I
have willingly to that end communicated
the ſame unto them."

The *Brief Catechiſm* is divided into ten
Chapters; treating, in ſucceſſion, of the
Scripture, or word of God; of God; of
Jeſus Chriſt; of the Holy Spirit and of
the Trinity; of the Death, Reſurrection,
Aſcenſion and Exaltation of *Chriſt*; of

F 5   Mort-

Mortification and Holinefs; of the Commandments, and fo of love to God and Men; of Faith; of the Church; of the Refurrection of the dead, and of the laft Judgement.

Thefe Catechifms alarmed the advocates for the orthodox Faith; and the authority of the fcripture language and declarations, under which the writers took fhelter, was infufficient to protect him from a profecution, and his book from an ignominious cenfure.

The Parliament condemned, in particular, thofe Propofitions: (1.) " That God is confined to a certain place. (2.) That he has a bodily fhape. (3.) That he has paffions. (4.) That he is neither omnipotent nor unchangeable. (5.) That we are not to believe three perfons in the Godhead. (6.) That Jefus Chrift has not the nature of God, but only a divine Lordfhip. (7.) That he was not a prieft while upon earth, nor did reconcile men

to

to God. And (8.) That there is no Deity in the Holy Ghoſt*.

Conſidering the very limited ſtate of Free-Enquiry, at that time, it is rather ſurpriſing that a ninth propoſition, or ground of charge againſt Mr. *Biddle* had not been added; viz. the future annihilation of the wicked, or that they would not, as the godly and faithful, " live for ever," but be " deſtroyed, corrupted, burnt up, devoured, ſlain, paſs away and periſh." For he produced many texts to exhibit this view of future puniſhments.

The Propoſitions, which they did deduce from theſe catechetical pieces, were deemed ſufficient grounds for proceeding, with ſeverity, againſt Mr. *Biddle.* A learned, modern writer, who does not adopt the author's peculiar ſentiments, has obſerved of " the Scripture Catechiſm ;'" that it diſcovers an enlargement of mind,

* NEAL's Hiſtory of the PURITANS, V. 4. p. 135. 8vo.

a libea liberality of fentiment, and a fincerity in freely publifhing what he apprehended to be truth, which do honour to his memory *." But the age in which it was publifhed, as we have feen, was by no means difpofed to treat thofe compofitions or writers, that difcarded or oppofed the prevailing faith, with candor or equity. Of which Mr. *Biddle*, on this occafion, had new experience.

He was brought to the bar of the Houfe of Commons, which the Protector *Cromwell* had convened; and was examined whether he was the author of that *two-fold Scripture Catechifm*, wherein all the queftions are anfwered in the words of Scripture at large. Mr. *Biddle*, to thefe interrogatories, wifely made a reply, which, at once conveyed an appeal to the principles of equity, and expreffed his juft expectations from the genius of the Englifh conftitution. For he anfwered by afking, " Whether it feemed reafonable that one

* HARWOOD, of the Socinian Scheme, p. 21.

brought

brought before a judgment feat as a Criminal, fhould accufe himfelf?" The reafon, which this anfwer carried in it, was not admitted as a bar to the proceedings againft him; but on the 3d of *December*, he was committed clofe prifoner to the Gate-Houfe, and forbidden the ufe of pen, ink and paper, and denied the accefs of any vifitant.

In this cafe, nothing lefs than a capital judgement was to be expected; a Bill was accordingly brought in for punifhing him. In this fituation Mr. *Biddle* preferved a compofed and cheerful mind, and maintained his hope of an happy event from the providence of God, in whofe caufe he fuffered. His hope did not fail him; for the Protector, induced by reafons drawn from his own intereft, diffolved the Parliament, and the prifoner, after ten months imprifonment, obtained his liberty, *May* 28, by due courfe of law *.

* Unitarian Tracts, V. 1. 4to. The Life of Biddle, p. 7. and BRITISH BIOGRAPHY, V. 6. 8vo. p. 86.

The

The resentment of government pursued the book as well as the author, for
an order was issued out, that the Catechism should be burnt by the hands of
the Common Hangman; which was accordingly done on the 14th of *December*.
This mode of casting an odium upon particular writings, hath been practised by
all governments, and in all ages *. The
disgrace ultimately falls on those who
adopt this measure. For it indicates the
weakness of their cause, or the indolence
of its partisans. They either have not
the ability, or will not be at the pains to
discuss and refute the opinions they would
suppress. It is a method of dismissing
as much within the power of the ignorant
as the learned; and of the fool as of the
wise man. And, after all, though a book
may be burnt, an impression cannot be
annihilated in one fire. Copies will be

* Cicero de naturâ Deorum, curâ Davisii, L.
1. c. 23. Minutius Felix, curâ Davisii, cap. 8.
Taciti Annales, L. 4. cap. 35.

secretly

secretly preserved and read; and will, in a future unprejudiced age, **bring** forward **the** question, if it hath been judiciously stated, and closely argued, to disgrace **the** memory of those who would have **stifled** enquiry.

It is however **but justice** to the times of which we write to say, that while the ruling powers prosecuted and imprisoned **Mr.** *Biddle*, and burnt **his** Catechisms, some pursued a more fair and rational mode of exposing the supposed **weakness** of his arguments, and investigating **the** truth **of** his opinions. **Mr.** *Nicholas* **E***st-wick*, of *Wakton*, in *Northamptonshire*, and some time Fellow of Christ's **College**, in Cambridge, published a professed Examination and **Confutation of Mr.** *Biddle*'s Confession of Faith concerning the **Holy** Trinity. And to the **honour of** the leading men **in the** state, it should be mentioned, that they availed themselves **of the** learning and abilities of the celebrated **Dr.** *Owen* to discuss, from the press, **the po**sitions of **Mr.** *Biddle*'s Catechisms. **For**

at

at the command of the Right Honourable the Council of State, he drew up and publiſhed his VINDICIÆ EVANGELICÆ; or the Myſtery of the Goſpel vindicated, and Socinianiſm examined in the Conſideration and Confutation of a Catechiſm, called a *Scripture Catechiſm*, written by *J. Biddle*, A. M. Mr. *Neal* has called this work a learned and elaborate Treatiſe. The celebrity of Mr. *Biddle*'s writings was not confined to England, they were attended to abroad, and ſeveral Foreigners publiſhed Refutations of his ſentiments *.

Another effect of Mr. *Biddle*'s Catechetical publication was, that to guard the minds of people, eſpecially of the riſing generation, from what were deemed heretical ſentiments, the provincial Aſſembly at *London*, publiſhed an Exhortation to Catechiſing, with directions for the more regular conducting of it. Theſe inſtructions were ſent to the ſeveral Claſſes of *London*, and after their example the aſſo-

* Bock Hiſtoria Antitrinitanorum, Tom. 1. Par. 1. p. 54.

ciated

ciated Minifters in the feveral Counties of England, publifhed the like exhortation to their Brethren *.

This meafure originated from zeal for a particular fyftem, and certainly tended to fix in young minds ftrong prejudices in its favour; yet it was worthy of true piety and zeal, and may be fuppofed to have greatly contributed to prevent a pernicious and total ignorance of all religious principles.

* NEAL's Hiftory of the Puritans, V. 4. p. 135, 6. 8vo.

SECTION

SECTION IX.

A new profecution commenced againſt Mr.
Biddle.

IT may be thought, that after having experienced ſuch evils and ſufferings for the open **avowal** and defence of his religious opinions, Mr. *Biddle* ſhould have withdrawn from public **notice, and have** ſilently enjoyed his **own** view of things **in** private. The love of eaſe and ſafety would certainly **have** dictated this conduct, and worldly prudence would have approved it. But Mr. *Biddle* ſeems to have entertained other ſentiments, and to have thought, that perſonal comfort and ſafety ought to be ſacrificed to truth and our duty to God. *Socrates,* the Grecian Sage, thought ſo before him[*]. When he was

pleading

---

[*] Ἴσως ουν αν τις εἴποι, Σιγῶν τε ϰ ἡσυχιαν αγων, ω Σωκρατες, ουχ οιος τ' ἐση ἡμιν ἐξελθων ζην; Τουτι δη ἐστι παντων

pleading before his judges: " Perhaps,"
says he, " some one will afk, why can you
" not, *Socrates*, withdraw, and banifhing
" yourfelf from us, fpend your life in
" filent and retired leifure? It would be
" a moft difficult matter to convince you
" that I cannot do this. Should I urge,
" that this would be to difobey God, and
" that therefore I cannot be filent, you
" would difcredit me, as a Diffembler.
" Were I to alledge, that to hold daily
" converfations on virtue and other topics,
" which you have heard that I canvas
" and inveftigate with others, is the greateft

ταυλων χαλιπαλαλιν πισαι τινας υμων. ιαιτι γαρ λιγω,
δι τω θιω απιιθων τιυτ᾽ ιςι, και δια τουλ᾽ αδυνατον
πουχιαν αγιιν, ου πισιςθι μοι, ως ιιρωνιυομινω᾽ ιαν τ᾽
αυθις λιγω, δι κỳ τυγχανιι μιγιςον αγαθον ανθρωπω τουλο,
ικαςης ημιρας πιρι αριτης τους λογους ποιισθαι, κỳ των
αλλων, πιρι ων υμεις ιμου ηκουλι διαλιγομινι, κỳ ιμαυλον
κỳ αλλους ιξιταζοντος (ὁδε ανιξιταςος βιος, ου βιωτος
ανθρωπω) ταυλα δ᾽ιτι ηλον πισιςθι μοι λιγονλι. τα δι
ιχιι μιν ουλως, ως ιγω φημι, ω ανδρις, πιιθιιν δι ου ραδια.
Platonis Dialog. V. curà Forfter, p. 111, 112, &
Opera Platonis, quoted by Dr. Doddridge. Family Expofitor, vol. 3. on Acts iv. 19. note (n).

" human

" human felicity ; for a life fpent without
" enquiry is not a life for man: you would
" be as far from believing me.   But
" things are as I reprefent them, though
" it is not eafy to perfuade you of it.
" If ye would difmifs me and fpare my
" life, on condition that I fhould leave off
" to teach my fellow-citizens, I would ra-
" ther die a thoufand times than accept
" the propofal."

Mr. *Biddle's* conduct had a fuperior
fanction in that of the Apoftles ; who,
when commanded by the Jewifh Sanhe-
drim, not to fpeak at all, nor teach in the
name of *Jefus*, anfwered, " Whether it
" be right in the fight of God, to hearken
" unto you more than unto God, judge
" ye." Acts 4. 19.   A Chriftian has more
powerful reafons for a ftrict, open and firm
attachment to truth than has an heathen
philofopher ; for he has the word of God
to direct his enquiries, and authorife his
conduct, and he has the hope of immor-
tality to fupport and animate his fteady
zeal.

Mr.

Mr. *Biddle,* influenced by thefe confiderations, fo far from withdrawing from
the fcene of exertion and fuffering, betook
himfelf to his former exercifes for propagating, what appeared to his mind, divine
truth, as clofely connected with the honour
of Almighty God. Scarcely therefore had
a year expired, after he was releafed from
the profecution on account of his *Scripture Catechifm,* than a new danger, not
lefs formidable, overtook him.

Notwithftanding the odium, under which
his fentiments laid, and the offence they
gave to the governing power, they began
to be embraced by a confiderable part of
a Baptift Congregation under the paftoral
care of Mr. *Griffin;* who took alarm at
this infection, and to ftop its fpread, challenged Mr. *Biddle* to a public difputation
in his Meeting-houfe at St. *Paul's.* Mr.
Neal has, to whatever caufe it was owing,
given a reprefentation of this matter not
quite fo honourable to Mr. *Biddle,* as the
truth of the fact requires, for he fays,
that

that Mr. *Biddle*, being of a reftlefs fpirit, challenged Mr. *Griffin*; thus not only miftating the proceedings, as originating from Mr. *Biddle*, but uncandidly afcribing them to a wrong caufe. It appears from Mr. *Biddle*'s Biographer, that he not only was not firft in this bufinefs, but waved the challenge, and declined the difputation for fome time. At length he met Mr. *Griffin*, amidft a numerous auditory, among whom were many of his bitter and fiery Adverfaries, efpecially fome Bookfellers, notorioufly known for their falfe zeal and former oppofition to Chriftian liberty, under the name of *Beacon Friers* *.

To introduce the debate, Mr. *Griffin* afked, " If any man there did deny, that *Chrift* was God Moft High ?" The event gave too much reafon to apprehend, that the matter was thus opened, infidioufly to draw from Mr. *Biddle*'s own mouth,

---

* Neal's Hiftory of the Puritans, V. 4. p. 137. 8vo. Their names were Thomas Underhill, Luke Fawn and Nathaniel Webb. See *Crofby*'s Hiftory of the *Englifh Baptifts*, V. 1. p. 209.

grounds

grounds of accufation. **Mr.** *Biddle*, with fincerity and firmnefs, replied, " I do deny it." **Mr.** *Griffin*, on this, it fhould feem, entered into a proof of the affirmative ; but, in the judgement of judicious hearers, was not able to fupport his caufe againft Mr. *Biddle* ; and the difputation was adjourned to another day, when **Mr.** *Biddle*, it **was** agreed, fhould take his turn of eftablifhing the negative fide of the queftion between them.

Before that day came, other meafures of confutation, befides fair difcuffion and argument, were adopted. The Adverfaries of **Mr.** *Biddle* laid hold of the open and generous profeffion he had made **of** his fentiments : information was lodged againft him. He was apprehended and committed to the *Compter*, **July 3, 1655 ;** from thence he was removed to *Newgate*, and was at the next Seffions called to trial for his life, on the Ordinance againft Blafphemy and Herefy, which we have before mentioned. The iniquity of this proceeding **was** aggravated by its being **founded** on

on an act, which had never properly received the force of a law, and had, for
feveral years, lain obfolete. But the in-
veterate zeal of perfecutors admits no meafures of kindnefs or equity. The manner
of conducting this profecution againft Mr.
Biddle, as well as the grounds on which
it was commenced, afforded a proof of
this. For when he prayed, that Counfel
might be allowed him to plead the ille-
gality of the indictment, it was denied
him by the judges, and the fentence of a
mute threatened. Upon this he gave into
Court his exceptions engroffed on parch-
ment, and with much ftruggling had Counfel allowed him ; but the trial was deferred
to the next day.

In this emergency, the principles and
policy of *Oliver Cromwell* operated in favour of Mr. *Biddle*. The *Protector* was
an enemy to perfecution ; and among the
capital articles, on which his government,
was formed, were thefe liberal ones, viz.
" That fuch as profefs faith in God by
Jefus Chrift, (though differing in judgement

ment from the doctrine, worship or discipline publicly held forth) shall not be
restrained from, but shall be protected in
the profession of the faith, and exercise of
their religion ; and that all laws, statutes
and ordinances, &c. to the contrary of the
aforesaid liberty, shall be esteemed null and
void. It was also his art, by dexterous
management, to keep the opposite parties
then in the nation in a kind of equipoise,
which he found necessary for his own security. He saw it was not for the interest
of his government to have Mr. *Biddle*
either condemned or absolved. He therefore took him out of the hands of the law,
and detained him in prison. His release
would have offended the *Presbyterians* and
all the enemies to religious liberty, of
whom there appeared a great number at
his trial. On the contrary, the proceedings against Mr. *Biddle* were opposed by
the friends of liberty ; they were censured
and reprobated by different publications
from the press. And while petitions were,
by one party presented against him, the

G   other

other did not lie dormant, but folicited his difcharge, and urged their fuit by pointed remonftrances againft that Ordinance, as threatening all their liberties, and infringing the fundamental Articles of the *Protector*'s government. Many Congregations of *Baptifts* appeared, on this occafion, as Friends to Mr. *Biddle*, and Advocates for the rights of Confcience. At length Cromwell, wearied with petitions, for and againft, to terminate the affair, and, in fome degree meet the wifhes of each party, banifhed Mr. *Biddle* to the Ifle of Scilly, whither he was fent *October* 5, 1655 *.

Difagreeable and afflictive, as muft be this ftate of Exile, it was rather a fhelter from the vindictive fpirit of his enemies, and was a means of preventing another Parliament, under the Protector, from decreeing any thing more rigid againft him, as

* Short Account of the Life of John Biddle, p. 7, 8. and CROSBY's Hiftory of the Englifh Baptifts, vol. 1. p. 206. 215.

he

he was abfent and out of their way. The inconveniences and wants of his fituation were alfo relieved by the kindnefs of the *Protector* himfelf; who, after fome time, allowed him in his Exile an hundred crowns per annum for his fubfiftence; which, as an act of pure generofity, fhewn to a perfecuted man, whofe tenets could not be agreeable to *Cromwell*, reflects honour on his name.

The evils of Mr. *Biddle*'s banifhment were, in other refpects, alleviated; efpecially by the ftate of his mind, and the employment of his thoughts. " Here, his Biographer informs us, he enjoyed much divine comfort from the heavenly contemplations, for which his retirement gave him opportunity. Here he had fweet communion with the Father and his Son *Jefus Chrift*, and attained, in many particulars, a clearer underftanding of the divine Oracles. Here, whilft he was more abundantly confirmed in the doctrines of his Confeffion of Faith, &c. yet he feems,

G 2   notwith-

notwithſtanding, to have become more doubtful about ſome other points which he formerly held; as appears from his *Eſſay to explaining the Revelation*, which he wrote after his return thence; which ſhews that he ſtill maintained a free and unprejudiced mind *.

Though Mr. *Biddle*'s baniſhment laſted three years, his friends were not regardleſs of his intereſt and liberty; but were active in their endeavours to procure his releaſe. He himſelf wrote letters, both to the Protector and to Mr. *Calamy*, an eminent Preſbyterian Miniſter, to reaſon them into compaſſion, but without immediate ſucceſs. It may, perhaps, be offered in extenuation of Mr. *Calamy*'s apparent neglect of Mr. *Biddle*'s applications, that in *Oliver*'s time he kept himſelf as private as he could. At length, the ſolicitations of friends, favoured by the opera-

* A ſhort Account, &c. p. 8. PALMER's Nonconformiſt's Memorial, v. 1. p. 74.

tion

tion of other occurences, prevailed, and
the Protector permitted a writ of *Habeas
Corpus* to be granted out of the Upper-
Bench Court, whereby Mr. *Biddle* was
brought back, and by that Court fet at
liberty, as finding no legal caufe of de-
taining him.

SECTION X.

His renewal of his public Miniſtrations— his laſt impriſonment—and Death.

THE reflexions with which we opened the preceding chapter, are equally pertinent to the conduct of Mr. *Biddle*, which we are to review in this. He ſtill preſerved the firmneſs of his mind. He ſtill felt the ardor of zeal. Notwithſtanding the dangers, ſufferings, and perſecutions, which he had ſuſtained, he was not terrified from what he counted his duty to *Chriſt*, in propagating the true knowledge of the only True God, and of *Jeſus Chriſt*, whom he had ſent. Upon his return to *London*, he reſumed his religious exerciſes among his friends, and acted as Paſtor to a Congregation in the City, formed

formed on the principles of the Independents *.

The national affairs foon took a turn unfavourable to Mr. *Biddle*'s profecution of his delightful work. For, about five months after, the *Protector* died, and *Richard* fucceeding, called a Parliament, which, it was fuppofed, would be particularly inimical to him. At the importunity of a noble friend, he reluctantly retired into the Country, during their feffion. On the diffolution of that Parliament, he returned to his former ftation.

This period of tranquillity, and of his minifterial fervices, was but of fhort duration. The enjoyment of religious liberty was, in thofe times, fluctuating and precarious, dependent upon the ftate of political affairs, and changing with the national revolutions. Of this Mr. *Biddle* had repeated experience. And though the reign of his enemies, the *Prefbyterians*, was now drawing to its clofe, its termina-

* Britifh Biography, 8vo. v. 6. p. 87.

tion

tion afforded him no fecurity; but, by the
change of government, he was involved in
new difficulties and dangers; and became
a fufferer in common with thofe, from
whofe hands he had a little before fuffered. With the fettlement of CHARLES
II. on the throne of his anceftors, the
antient government in the Church and
State was reftored. The *Prefbyterians* foon
felt the iron hand of power, and all Diffenters from the *Epifcopal* worfhip were
treated on the fame intolerant principles.
Their liberty was taken away, and their
meetings were punifhed as feditious.

Mr. *Biddle* endeavoured to avoid the
threatening ftorm, by reftraining himfelf
from public to more private affemblies.
But his prudence and caution were in-
effectual. The retired and peaceable affo-
ciations of himfelf and his adherents could
not elude the jealous eye of magiftracy
by their fecrecy, nor difarm its rage by
their harmleffnefs. For on the *firft* of
June, 1662, he was haled from his lodg-
ings, where he and fome few of his friends
were

were met for divine worſhip, and carried before Sir *Richard Brown*, a Juſtice of Peace, who committed them all to priſon, without admitting them to bail. Mr. *Biddle* was doomed to the dungeon, where he lay for five hours. The Recorder, actuated by more reverence for the law, releaſed them on giving ſecurity for anſwering, at the next ſeſſions, to the charge brought againſt them. They accordingly performed this. But the Court not being able to find any ſtatute whereon to form a criminal indictment, they were referred to the following ſeſſions, and then were proceeded againſt, under pretence of an offence at Common Law; a mode of conviction which leaves much to the breaſt of the judge. The deciſion, in this caſe, was, that every one of the Hearers ſhould be fined in the penalty of twenty pounds, and Mr. *Biddle* himſelf in one hundred; and they were ordered to lie in priſon till theſe mulcts were paid.

The Sheriff was diſpoſed to have remitted the greateſt part of Mr. *Biddle's*

penalty.

penalty, and to have accepted even ten
pounds, which he would have paid. Sir
Richard Browne rigorously infifted upon
the payment of the full fum, and even, in
that cafe, threatened him with a feven
years imprifonment, which occafioned his
continuing in prifon.

But in lefs than five weeks, through
the noifomenefs of the place, and the
want of air, which was peculiarly difgree-
able and pernicious to him, whofe only
recreation and exercife had been, for many
years, to walk daily in the frefh air, he
contracted a difeafe which was attended
with immediate danger to his life. So
unrelenting, fo unpitying is bigotry, Sir
R. Brown could not be moved, in this
extremity, to grant the fick prifoner the
comfort of a removal, in order to reco-
very. The Sheriff, whofe name was *Mey-
nel*, acted on the principles of humanity,
and granted it. But, on the fecond day
after, between five and fix o'clock in the
morning, the 22d of *September*, 1662,
he died, in the 47th year of his age.

He

He had formerly affured his friends, that he had brought himfelf, by frequent medi-tations on the refurrection and future happinefs, to look on death with contempt. The manner with which he met his diffolution, evinced to them the truth of thefe declarations. For, when by the difeafe more violently affecting his head, he perceived a great alteration, he fignified it to his friends, and abfolutely declined any further difcourfe; but compofed himfelf, as it were to fleep, for eight hours before he expired, being very fparing of words, or even of groans, that might argue any impatience. When a pious perfon, who attended him, broke forth into this valedictory wifh, *God grant that we may fee one another in the kingdom of heaven;* his fpeech failing him, he fhewed how pleafing that wifh was to him, by lifting up his quivering hand. He had, before this illnefs, frequently dropt expreffions, that indicated an expectation of his approaching end; often faying, that if he fhould be once more caft into prifon, he

fhould

should never be reftored to liberty; and moreover, *That the work was done*, meaning, that the Truth which he apprehended God had raifed him up to profefs, was fufficiently brought to light, and that there only wanted ingenuoufnefs in men, for the embracing and acknowledging it *.

* Short Account of his Life, p. 9.

SECTION

SECTION XI.

His Works, not noticed before.

IT has been our defign, in the preceding Sections, to bring into view
only thofe works of Mr. *Biddle,* which
raifed the public attention, or drew on
himfelf fevere profecutions. But, befides
thefe, there were other publications of his,
which were fpecimens of his learning and
genius, or expreffive of his zeal to promote religious enquiry and truth. His
juvenile performances have been before
mentioned.

During his banifhment to the *Ifle* of
Scilly, as we have faid, he drew up an Effay
to the *explaining of the Revelations.* In
which he treated of the beaft in the Apo-
calypfe, *Antichrift,* the *perfonal reign of*

2   *Chrift*

Chrift on the earth, &c. * His prefent Biographer not having been able to procure a fight of this piece, can fay nothing more concerning it.

In the year 1653, Mr. *Biddle* publifhed feveral fmall pieces, which were tranflations of Tracts written by fome of the *Polifh Unitarians*. Among thefe was one entitled *Brevis Difcuffio*; or a *Brief Enquiry touching a better way than is commonly made ufe of to refute* Papists, *and reduce* Protestants *to a Certainty and Unity in* religion. The Author of this Tract was *Joachim Stegman*, a *German*, who, on account of his attachment to the *Socinian* fentiments, was difmiffed from the paftoral office in two Churches of the Reformed; on which he went into *Poland*, and was firft chofen Principal of the Univerfity at *Racow*, and was then fent, by the Synod of *Racow*, to fucceed *Valentinus Radecius*,

---

* Short Account of his Life, p. 4. and Bri-tish Biography, 8vo. v. 6. p. 79. note (l) and p. 87.

as Paſtor of the *Unitarian* Church at *Clau-diopolis*, or, as it is called in German, *Clauſenburg*, in Saxony, where he died in 1633 *.

This ʼwork was printed in 1633, a tranſlation of it is preſerved in the *Phœnix*. It incurred cenſure, as containing ſundry *Socinian* and *Pelagian* tenets, and was aſcribed to Mr. *John Hales*, of *Eton*.

" The ſcope of it is to ſhew, that the Proteſtants, by adhering to the peculiar ſyſtem of *Luther*, *Brentius*, *Calvin*, *Beza*, &c. &c. had, in many inſtances, offered weak and improper arguments againſt Popery, which had laid them under needleſs difficulties. His advice is therefore to diſcard all human authority, and to ſtick to the ſcripture only, as explained and underſtood by right reaſon, without having any regard to tradition, or the authority of Fathers, Councils, &c.

* Bock Hiſtoria Antitrinitariorum, Tom. 1. p. II. p. 949, 950, et Sandii Bibliotheca Antitrin. p 132.

" Mr,

"Mr. *Bayle*, we are told, fays this book did more hurt than good, not becaufe it was not well written, but becaufe it tended to difparage the reputation of the firft Reformers, broke in upon their feveral fyftems, and, what was worfe than all the reft, was manifeftly the work of fomebody tainted with the herefies of *Socinus* and *Arminius* *."

We fuppofe that Mr. *Bayle* fpeaks here not his own opinion, but the fentiments of thofe who prefer the party they have once efpoufed to good fenfe and truth. The piece opens with this principle; "He that will refute an error, muft neither be entangled in the fame, nor reject the true grounds of Refutations. In the fucceeding chapters it treats of Fathers and Doctors; of the Holy Spirit; of the true Opinion touching the Judge; of Traditions; of Philofophical Principles; of the true Opinion touching the Rule; whether

* An Hiftorical View of the Controverfy concerning an Intermediate State. 2d ed. p. 64.

the

the dead do properly live; whether *Chrift* in heaven hath yet flefh and blood; whether it be poffible to obey the precepts of *Chrift*; and whether it be neceffary to obey the precepts of *Chrift*.

The eighth chapter of this work may be deemed curious, not only for the example it gives of the fupport which Popery derives from fome doctrines embraced by Proteftants, but for the full and yet concife view which it exhibits of the arguments againft an eftablifhed doctrine, on which few, even in the prefent day, venture to think with freedom. " *Luther* and *Calvin*," he obferves, " teach fuch things as are injurioufly defended not only againft the Papifts, but alfo againft the very life of the Chriftian religion, true piety. Of the former fort is that opinion wherein they hold that the dead live. It will feem abfurd, and indeed the thing itfelf is very abfurd; yet they believe it.

" For they fuppofe that the fouls of men, in that very moment wherein they are parted from their bodies by death,

are

are carried either to heaven, and do there feel heavenly joy, and poſſeſs all kinds of happineſs which God hath promiſed to his people; or to Hell, and are there tormented, and excruciated with unquenchable fire. And this, as was ſaid before, they attribute to the mere ſouls ſeparated from the bodies, even before the reſurrection of the men themſelves, that is to ſay, while they are yet dead. But theſe things cannot happen to any thing which is not alive, for that which doth not live, doth not feel; and conſequently neither enjoyeth pleaſure, nor endureth pain. Wherefore they believe, in effect, that the dead live; namely, in the ſame manner that they affirm *Peter*, *Paul*, and other dead men, to live in heaven.

" Now this is the foundation not only of Purgatory, but alſo of that horrible Idolatry practiſed amongſt the Papiſts, whilſt they invocate the Saints that are dead. Take this away, and there will be no place left for the others. To what purpoſe is the fire of Purgatory, if ſouls
                                                    ſeparated

feparated from the body feel nothing ?
To what purpofe are prayers to the Virgin
Mary, to *Peter*, and to *Paul*, and other
dead men, if they can neither hear prayers
nor intercede for you ? On the contrary,
if you admit this, you cannot eafily over-
throw the invocation of Saints. Now
though the thing be fuch of itfelf as deferves to feem abfurd to every one, yet
will we fee, whether the contrary thereof
be not fet down in the Scripture.

" Nor need we go far for an example,
fince we have a pregnant one in the argument of *Chrift*, wherein he proveth the
future refurrection of the dead from thence ;
that God is the God of *Abraham*, *Ifaac*
and *Jacob*, but is not the God of the dead,
but of the living ; whence he concludeth
that they live to God, that is, fhall be
recalled to life by God, that he may manifeft himfelf to be their God, or Benefactor. This argument would be fallacious, if before the Refurrection they felt
heavenly joy. For then God would be
their God or Benefactor, namely, according

ing to their fouls, although their bodies
fhould never rife again.

"In like manner, the reafoning of the
Apoftle would be fallacious, 1 Cor. 15.
30, 31, 32. wherein he proveth the Refurrection by that argument; becaufe,
otherwife, thofe that believe in *Chrift* would
in vain feek hazards every hour; in vain
fuffer fo many calamities for *Chrift*, which
he teacheth by his own example. Again,
becaufe otherwife it would be better to
fing the fong of the *Epicureans*, Let us
eat and drink, for to-morrow we fhall die.
In fhort, of all men Chriftians would be
moft miferable. Certainly this would be
falfe, if the godly prefently after death did
in their fouls enjoy celeftial happinefs, and
the wicked feel torment. For they would
not in vain fuffer calamities, nor thefe
follow the pleafures of the flefh fcotfree.
And the godly would be far happier than
the wicked.

"Since, therefore, it is the abfurdeft
thing in the world, to fay that *Chrift* and
the

the Apoſtle *Paul* did not argue rightly;
is it not clear that the doctrine is falſe,
which being granted, ſo great an abſurdity
would be charged on *Chriſt* and the Apoſtle
Paul.

  " Farthermore, why ſhould *Peter* de-
fer the ſalvation of ſouls to the laſt day,
1 Pet. 1. 5. *who are kept by the power
of God, through faith unto Salvation, ready
to be revealed in the laſt time*; and *Paul*
the crown of righteouſneſs to the day of
judgement; 2 Tim. 4. 8. *Henceforth there
is laid up for me a crown of righteouſneſs,
which the Lord, the righteous Judge, ſhall
give to me at that day, &c. ?*   To what
purpoſe ſhould the judgement be appointed?
How could it be ſaid of the godly under
the old Covenant, that they received not
the promiſe, God providing ſome better
things for us, that they might not without
us be made perfect. Heb. 11. 40. if the
ſoul of every one preſently after death,
even without the body, felt celeſtial happineſs.

                                   " But

" But the very nature of the thing itſelf refuſeth it. Is not living, dying, feeling, hearing, acting, proper to the whole man, or the compound of ſoul and body? Is not the body the inſtrument of the ſoul, without which it cannot perform her functions; as an artiſt knoweth indeed the art of working, but unleſs he have inſtruments at hand, he cannot produce any effect? Let the eye be ſhut, the ſoul will not ſee, though the power of ſeeing be not taken away from it. For as ſoon as you ſhall reſtore the inſtruments, a man will preſently ſee. Wherefore ſouls ſeparated from bodies, are neither dead nor live, and conſequently enjoy no pleaſure, and feel no pain. For thoſe things are proper to the whole compound.

" But the ſcripture ſaith, that the dead are not, that the ſpirit returneth to him that gave it; and of the ſpirits of the godly, that they are in the hand of God, but at the Reſurrection they ſhall be joined with the bodies; and then having gotten inſtru-

inftruments, they will put forth their opera-
tions."

The tranflation of this piece of *Stegman*'s is attended with a fhort preface, in
which Mr. *Biddle*, befides paffing enco-
miums on the work, chiefly labours to
obviate an objection that might be urged
againft it, from the ftrefs it lays on the
ufe of Reafon in religion. The remarks,
which Mr. *Biddle* offers on this point, are
worthy of attention.

Speaking of thofe who would be difpleafed with it, becaufe Reafon is therein
much cried up; he fays, " My defire
therefore is, that fuch perfons would but
confider what the Holy Scripture itfelf
faith on this behalf; namely, how *Paul*,
Rom. 12. 1. calleth the fervice which
Chriftians are to exhibit unto God, a *Rational* or *reafonable fervice.* And *Peter*, 1
Ep. 2. 2. ftileth the word of the Gofpel
which he preached, *fincere Rational Milk*
(for fo the original hath it, as any one who
is fkilled in that tongue, and looketh into the
Greek context, may perceive.) And ch.
3. 15.

3. 15. he faith, *Be ready always to make an apology unto every one that asketh you a Reason concerning the hope that is in you, with meeknefs and fear.* Which paffage clearly intimateth, that as there is no incongruity for others to require a *Reafon* of our hope in *Chrift*, fo we Chriftians are, above all other Profeffors whatfoever, obliged to be very *Rational*; for to make an apology or defence in the behalf of fo abftrufe and fublime a doctrine as ours is, requireth a more than ordinary improvement of *Reafon*.

" This being fo, it may feem ftrange why fo great a number even of *Proteftant* Minifters, fhould make *Reafon* a common theme to difclaim againft, giving to it (without warrant of Scripture) the name of *Corrupt Reafon* and *Carnal Reafon*, and others the like eulogies. But the truth is, they themfelves hold many abfurd, ridiculous, and *unreafonable* opinions, and fo know right well, that if men once begin to make ufe of their *Reafon*, and bring the Doctrines that are commonly taught to

the

the Touchſtone of the Scripture explained and managed in a rational way,
their Tenets and Reputation with the people will be ſoon laid in the duſt. Let
ſuch Miniſters henceforward either leave
off clamouring againſt *Reaſon*, or no more
open their mouths againſt Papiſts, and
their opinion about Tranſubſtantiation;
for whoſoever ſhall ſift the controverſy between *Papiſts* and *Proteſtants*, concerning
it, ſhall find that the principal, if not
only ground why we reject it, is becauſe
it is repugnant to *Reaſon*. But if Tranſubſtantiation is to be diſclaimed, becauſe
contrary to *Reaſon*, why ſhall not all
other *Unreaſonable* Doctrines upon the
ſame account be exploded, eſpecially ſeeing there is ſcarce any one of them can
plead ſo plauſible a colour of Scripture for
itſelf as that can?"

Another piece, tranſlated by Mr. *Biddle*,
was *Przipcovius'* Life of *Fauſtus Socinus*;
with the preliminary Diſcourſe prefixed
by that writer to the works of *Socinus*.
The Title of the Tract is, " *The* LIFE

of that incomparable Man, FAUSTUS SO-
CINUS SENENSIS, *deſcribed by a* POLO-
NIAN *Knight. Whereunto is added, an
excellent Diſcourſe which the ſame Author
would have had premiſed to the works of*
SOCINUS; *together with a Catalogue of
thoſe Works.* The views of Mr. *Biddle,*
in this publication, appear to have been
truly laudable and liberal, viz. to do
juſtice to a character which had been
much aſperſed, and to hold up, to contemplation, a great example; at the ſame
time that he enters a caveat againſt an implicit deference to the judgement of his
Hero.

" The life of *Socinus,* he ſays in his
preface, is here expoſed to thy view, that
by the peruſal thereof thou mayeſt receive
certain information concerning the man,
whom Miniſters and others traduce by
cuſtom; having (for the moſt part) never
heard any thing of his converſation, nor
ſeen any of his works, or if they have,
they were either unable or unwilling to

I   make

make a thorough fcrutiny into them, and
fo no marvel, if they fpeak evil of him.

" To fay any thing of him here, by
way of eulogy, as that he was one of the
moft pregnant wits that the world hath
produced; that none fince the Apoftles
hath deferved better of our Religion in
that the Lord *Chrift* hath chiefly made
ufe of his miniftry to retrieve fo many
precious truths of the Gofpel, which had
a long time been hidden from the eyes
of men by the artifice of Satan; that he
fhewed the world a more accurate way
to difcufs controverfies in Religion, and
to fetch out the very marrow of the Holy
Scripture, fo that a man may more avail
himfelf by reading his works, than perhaps by perufing all the Fathers, together
with the writings of more modern Authors; that the virtues of his will were
not inferior unto thofe of his underftanding, he being every way furnifhed to the
work of the Lord; that he opened the
right way to bring Chriftians to the unity
of the faith, and acknowledgment of the

fon

fon of God; that he took the fame courfe
to propagate the Gofpel, that *Chrift* and
the Apoftles had done before him, for-
faking his eftate and his neareft relations,
and undergoing all manner of labours and
hazards, to draw men to the knowledge
of the truth ; that he had no other end of
all his undertakings than the glory of God
and *Chrift*, and the falvation of himfelf
and others, it being impoffible for ca-
lumny itfelf with any colour to afperfe him
with the leaft fufpicion of worldly intereft ;
that he of all Interpreters explaineth the
precepts of *Chrift* in the ftrictteft manner,
and windeth up the lives of men to the
higheft ftrain of holinefs ; to fay the other
like things (though in themfelves true
and certain) would notwithftanding, here
be impertinent, in that it would foreftall
what the *Polonian* Knight hath written on
this fubject.

" To him, therefore, I refer thee, de-
firing thee to read his words without
prejudice, and then the works of *Socinus*
himfelf,

himself; and though thou beeft not thereby convinced that all which *Socinus* taught is true, (for neither am I myfelf of that belief, as having difcovered that in fome leffer things *Socinus*, as a man, went awry, however in the main he hit the truth) yet for fo much of *Chrift* as thou muft needs confefs appeareth in him, begin to have more favourable thoughts of him and his followers.

In addition to thefe pieces, which were Tranflations from *Polifh Unitarian* writers, we fhould add another Tract by the Knight who was the author of the former *, viz. *Differtatio de Pace*, &c. Or, a Discourse touching the Peace and Concord of the Church. *Wherein is elegantly and acutely argued, that not fo much a bad opinion, as a bad life, excludes a Chriftian out of the kingdom of heaven; and that the things neceffary to be known for the at-*

---

* For an Account of Przipcovius, we refer to Memoirs of the Life, &c. of Fauftus Socinus, p. 439—452.

tainment

tainment of falvation, are very few and easy; and finally, that those who pass amongst us under the name of Hereticks, are notwithstanding to be tolerated. This piece, written when the Author was little more than eighteen years old, had the honour of being ascribed to *Epifcopius.* The compofition is infinuating and masterly. The defign of it was liberal, and, confidering that the author did not agree, in their difcriminating opinion, with those on whofe behalf he wrote, it was peculiarly expreffive of generofity and candor. His view was to moderate the zeal and bitternefs, of which the *Socinians* were, in general, the unmerited objects. To effect this purpofe, it was introduced with fome reflexions on the lot of truth and innocence in this world. In fome following chapters is fhewn, what things concerning God and *Chrift* are neceffary to be known unto falvation, and what are the parts of true Faith; that fincere love towards God and *Chrift* is fufficient to Salvation, and that

the

the fame may be in thofe who err; that though faith and the Holy Spirit be the gifts of God, yet erring perfons have and may have them; that nothing but difobedience and unbelief exclude a man from eternal Salvation; and that fuch as err, are free from thefe; that the things neceffary to be known unto falvation are few and very fimple, and eafy to be underftood by the fimpleft; fuch is not the common doctrine concerning the Trinity; that there is not in this life a perfect knowledge of God, and of divine Myfteries, but in the other life; and that Faith, Hope and Charity are fufficient to Salvation. The difcuffion of thefe points is followed with a general Apology for *Socinians* on this principle, that they are not of fuch a perfuafion out of ambition, avarice, pleafure, or fuperftition, nor offend out of any malice, but only out of the care of their Salvation. Then follows an anfwer to the objection, drawn from their rejecting the confent of the Church, and refting the

defence

defence of their opinion upon the authority of Scripture only. This is succeeded by an answer to three other objections, with a comparison of *Calvin*'s Doctrine on Predestination, with the doctrine of others. Then some particular reasons for tolerating Heretics are offered; and the question, Who are true Heretics, is considered. The Tract concludes with an enquiry, what Heretics are to be excommunicated, and what not, and with a fuller Apology for those who in that age passed as such.

Mr. *Biddle*'s preface, which is a short one, concludes with that serious and just exhortation, formed on the most enlarged principles, which we have quoted, p. 10.

Large and numerous quotations from this work might be deemed tedious, and superseded by modern publications on the side of candor and moderation. But a passage or two, it is hoped, will not be unacceptable to the reader. To a prejudice imbibed against the *Socinian* sentiment

ment concerning the perſon of Chriſt, as
what muſt be highly diſpleaſing to him,
becauſe derogatory from his glory, the
Author anſwers thus : " The greateſt part
of them, who at this day recede from the
common ſenſe of the Church in ſo great
a matter, are not out of any raſhneſs ſo
perſuaded touching the Son of God, but
rather out of a pious fear, leſt they ſhould
detract from the Father ſomewhat of his
honour. Wherein if they unwittingly
offend againſt the Son, out of love to the
Father, (ſo that improbity mingle not itſelf with their error) it ſeemeth very cre-
dible, that the Son will, for the very love
of the Father, forgive them this error.
For he gave a notable proof of his meek-
neſs, when he prayed for his ignorant
murderers. What, think we, will not he
do for the love of the Father, who for the
love of men forgave ſo great an injury to
his enemies? Now if he out of love to
mankind doubted not to aſſume the form
of a ſervant, and really to endure extreme

diſgraces,

difgraces, certainly he will bear with the errors of men, who do not conceive worthily enough of his majefty and dignity, efpecially that which is paft. Will he, who for the fake of men, did of his own accord debafe himfelf to the loweft condition, punifh them for this very thing, namely, becaufe they out of ignorance, think more meanly of his condition than is fit? Efpecially when he himfelf, by his debafement, did in a manner give an occafion of fuch ignorance. Certainly it is incredible, that he who of his own accord underwent, for the fins of men, a reproachful kind of death, will not pardon to human weaknefs, a fimple opinion that derogates fomething from his antient excellence, if fo be the error be harmlefs, and be removed from all fin of malice."

Another paffage, in which he endeavours to remove the objection againft an indulgence to thofe who hold certain opinions, drawn from the fear, that the intereft,

tereſt of truth will ſuffer by the favour
ſhown to the erroneous, deſerves to be
quoted. " If," ſaith he, " we be afraid
of the contagion of ſuch errors, either in
behalf of ourſelves, or rather of the weaker
ones, in the firſt place we may not thereupon renounce brotherly love, which we
owe to them, although they err. For we
ought not to forſake a certain and clear
duty, leſt an uncertain evil ſhould happen,
nor to purſue even the moſt holy ends by
unlawful means. But, ſecondly, that fear
is vain. For if we have not the truth,
there is little danger to be feared from
them, much leſs if we have it. For ſince
they maintain their tenets with no arms,
nor with any force, and think it not ſo
much as lawful ſo to do, nor ſet them off
with any carnal allurements, certainly the
truth can never be by them either oppreſſed
with force, or overthrown with fraud, in-
aſmuch as the nature of truth is ſuch,
that like to eagles feathers, ſhe devoureth
all other light plumage of opinions, never

H 6   with-

withdrawing herself from us, unless she be tired either with our servitude, or sins. Which twain being not to be feared by us in a modest liberty of dissenting, and study of true charity, what cause is there why we should so warily fence our opinions from their tenets?

" Let us rather be possessed with a certain hope, that as earthen vessels being joined with those of tin or silver, are broken to pieces; so also if God, the Author of peace, shall bring back into the Church that happy tolerance, all false opinions fighting hand to hand with the true, will be dashed to shivers, and perish. Otherwise if we so much fear that mutual patience and friendly conference, we do not think well enough concerning the goodness of our cause.

" Heretofore, when the dawning of Gospel-light was returned, *Luther* and his followers would have wished that they might be tolerated in the communion of the *Roman* Church. But it concerned the

2   Pope

Pope to fecure his darknefs from the approach of the morning. Again, when a diffenfion was rifen up between the *Lutherans* and the *Reformed*, who was it that refufed the form of agreement that was offered, but he that doubted of his caufe? Now alfo in the very reformed Church itfelf, upon the diffenfion concerning Fate, none are more difpleafed with tolerance, than they that fufpect the truth of this doctrine. Would error were fo circumfpect in the cradle of its infancy, as it is provident being once grown up. But it being blind when it is born, doth afterward become fharp-fighted, forefeeing its fate afar off, and efchewing it, and is never more ingenious to prolong its life, than when it is preffed with the confcience of its own weaknefs."

In aid of the defign and reafonings of this Tract, Mr. *Biddle* added a Poftfcript; in which, among other reflexions, are the following pertinent remarks and clofe appeals to thofe who, arrogating to

themfelves

themfelves the character of the Orthodox, cenfure all others as Heretics.

Mr. *Biddle* granting, that he who contradicts the divine writings of the Apoftles, fhould be no lefs efteemed an Heretic, than he who oppofed the Apoftles preaching by word of mouth, adds, " but even thus can we not challenge that cenforian rod againft Heretics, (referring to certain particular paffages in the Epiftles.) For they whom ye place in the rank of Heretics, are fo far from contradicting the Holy Scripture, that they wage war againft you out of the fame, and appeal to the judgement thereof, not without a certain hope of victory, in the examination of their caufe, inafmuch as they embrace the Scripture in all things, with as great veneration of mind as you do; nor amongft all the Chriftian Churches, which are at this day extant, fhall ye fhew any one (that I know of) which doth not religioufly, and from the heart, yield an undoubted affent to all thofe things, that are propofed and taught

taught in the Holy Scripture. Wherefore there is no caufe why ye fhould condemn any one of them for Herefy, fince they agree with you in giving due credence to the facred writ. And therefore whatfoever pretence ye feek for your carnal zeal againft fuch as you call Heretics, yet to indifferent judgements can no other ground hereof appear, than their diffent from your interpretation of the Holy Scripture, as to the controverted doctrines.

" But I will here bountifully grant you, that ye have in all things hit the true fenfe of the Scripture, and defend it. Neverthelefs, it is further requifite, that ye make this plain to them, whom ye brand with the crime of Herefy. But what here is the ftrefs of your arguments? Ye appeal again to the Holy Scripture, and from thence condemn Heretics. But they have already ftricken this weapon out of your hands, fhewing that the Holy Scripture maketh for you, only in your own fenfe and

and interpretation, and that they are accordingly condemned by you, not from the facred Scripture, but from your interpretation of the facred Scripture. And this is the circle of your arguing, which they defervedly reject.

" Draw out therefore againſt Heretics thoſe truly apoſtolical weapons, not the *Thraſonical* prating of the Chair in the Univerſity, but the power of the Holy Spirit, wherewith the Apoſtles being indued, could deliver Blaſphemers to Satan, 1 Tim. 1. 10. and flay Hypocrites with the ſpeaking of a word, Acts 5. If ye want the powerful efficacy of this ſpirit, acknowledge your raſhneſs and iniquity in condemning them, to whom ye are not able, with evident and ſufficient arguments to demonſtrate your interpretation of the Holy Scripture, and who by the fame right, and from the fame foundation object to you not only errors, but alſo hereſies.

" Ye

" Ye know that of *Chrift*, *condemn not, and ye fhall not be condemned.* What account will ye give to this juft Judge, for fo often violating this precept? Your zeal of the divine glory will not then excufe you; for though it palliate itfelf under this reverend name, yet is it wholly of the flefh, and odious to God. But if ye affirm, that it proceedeth from the Holy Spirit, produce arguments worthy of fo great an Author. For neither is this Spirit fo weak, but that he can fhew forth tokens of his divine authority and prefence in his Minifters, and by them againft his enemies. But whither am I carried away? I befeech thee, good reader, to pardon this digreffion of mine; and having liked the pious counfel of our Author, intreat God that he would inftil into other readers alfo a mind ftudious of peace and concord.

Such fentiments are fo important and liberal, that they can fcarcely be repeated too often, or be prefented in too various forms.

forms. For every reprefentation, whether in a modern or antient drefs, carries
a recommendation of them to every candid mind, and it may be prefumed, will
not be wholly without effect in making
them to be known, approved and felt.

SECTION

SECTION XII.

His Character.

WE have traced Mr. *Biddle* through the labours, &c. of a ſtudious, and the events of an afflicted life. His ſtudies were devoted to the purſuit of religious knowledge, and his ſufferings were incurred by a conſcientious adherence to the convictions which his enquiries produced. From both the reader will form his own ideas concerning his abilities, learning and character. They were all held in high eſtimation by thoſe who perſonally knew him, and were acknowledged by his enemies.

His acquaintance with the Holy Scriptures, as was obſerved in the ſecond Section, was ſingularly comprehenſive and exact. His knowledge of them was in-
ſtead

stead of a Concordance, for no part could be named, but he would presently cite the book, chapter, and verse. This perfect knowledge in the Scriptures, joined with an happy and ready memory, whereby he had, at recollection, what he had read in other authors, gave him a great advantage in all debates, of which, without the least ostentation, he availed himself.

The distinguishing point of view, under which the preceding account exhibits him, is that of a REFORMER, and a sufferer for conscience sake : yet, in the former character, he appears to have been modest and candid, and in the latter patient and resigned. " It was," says his Biographer, who appears to have been intimately acquainted with him, " in his heart to promote piety, and he had no design to aggrandise his name by opposition to common doctrines. Indeed, he was a great asserter of common doctrines against novel opinions, that tended either to sedition, libertinism, or superstition. And

in

in what he held contrary to the current, he did not endeavour to tie thofe he had won, to be of his mind in fuch a fociety, and by fuch a fociety, and by fuch bands, as might continue them a fucceffive party, bearing his name as their Founder; but left them to all that liberty, which the duty of owning the truth according to their confcience, and of mutual edification would allow them *."

Zealous and active as Mr. *Biddle* was in promoting what he deemed great and important Truth, he was ftill more zealous in promoting holinefs of life and manners; for this was always his end and defign in what he taught. " He valued not his doctrines for fpeculation, but practice, infomuch that he would not difcourfe of thofe points wherein he differed from others, with thofe that appeared not religious according to knowledge. Neither could he bear thofe that

---

* Short Account of his Life, p. 10.

diffembled

diffembled in profeffion for worldly interefts."

His own life was pure and irreproach-
able. Mr. *Anthony Wood* acknowledges,
that, " except his opinions, there was
little or nothing blame-worthy in him."
He was fo free from being queftioned for
any the leaft blemifh in his life, that one
of his Advocates fays, " the *Informers*
themfelves, who brought on the laft profecution againft him, had been heard to
admire his ftrict exemplary life," full of
modefty, fobriety, and forbearance, no ways
contentious, touching the great things of
the world, but altogether taken up with
the great things of God, revealed in the
Holy Scriptures *.

Another writer, on the proceedings a-
gainft him, gives this teftimony to his
converfation. " We have," fays he, " had
intimate knowledge thereof for fome years;
but we think he needs not us, but may
appeal even to his enemies, for his vin-

* Short Account of his Life, p. 10.

dication

dication therein. Let thofe that knew
him at *Oxford* for the fpace of feven or
eight years, thofe that knew him at *Gloucefter* about three years, thofe that knew
him at *London* thefe eight or nine years,
(moft of which he hath been a prifoner)
fpeak what they know, of unrighteoufnefs,
uncleannefs, unpeaceablenefs, malice, pride,
profanenefs, drunkennefs, or any the like
iniquity, which they can accufe him of,
or hath he, (as the manner of Heretics
is) 2 Pet. 2. 3. *Through covetoufnefs with
feigned words made merchandife of any?*
Hath he not herein walked upon fuch true
grounds of Chriftian felf-denial, that none
in the world can ftand more clear and
blamelefs herein alfo? He having fhunned
to make any of thofe advantages which
are eafily made in the world, by men of
his parts and breeding, languages, and
learning, that (if any known to us) he
may truly fay as the Apoftle, *I have coveted
no man's filver, or gold, or apparel; yea, ye
yourfelves know, that thefe hands have
miniftered to my neceffities;* he ever account-
ing

ing it *a more bleſſed thing to give than to receive* †."

It is a proof of the great and ſerious regard which he had for univerſal righteouſneſs: that " he would often tell his friends, that no religion could benefit a bad man ; and call upon them to reſolve with themſelves, as well to profeſs and practiſe the truth that is according to godlineſs, as to ſtudy to find it out, and that againſt all terrors and allurements to the contrary ; being aſſured that nothing diſpleaſing to Almighty God, would be any wiſe profitable to them *. The probity of his own conduct was eminently conſpicuous: ſo that the appeal was made to many perſons of worth and credit in London, on the juſtice and integrity of his heart, and on his holy care not to diſſemble, play the hypocrite, or deal fraudulently with any, not even to ſave his life ‡.

† Crosby's Hiſtory of the Engliſh Baptiſts, vol. 1. p. 210, 11, 12.

* Short Account of his Life, p. 10.

‡ Croſby's Hiſtory of the Engliſh Baptiſts. V. 1. p. 210, 211.

The

The foundation of his moral excellencies was laid, where the foundation of every good attainment muſt be laid, in the application of the earlieſt years to the purſuit of divine wiſdom. Before he left ſchool, there was diſcovered in him " a ſingular piety of mind, and contempt of ſecular affairs :" he applied himſelf to the ſtudy of virtue, together with the ſtudy of literature and ſcience : and, in his younger years, was an amiable example of filial affection to his Mother, to whom, becoming a widow by the death of his Father, he, with great diligence, gave dutiful aſſiſtance *.

The events, which we have ſurveyed, furniſh a ſtriking proof of the perſeverance and fortitude, with which he followed truth, and met his ſufferings. And, though he was converſant in the diſcuſſion of points, involved, by the inventions of men, and a mixture of human ſcience, in great difficulties and obſcurity, yet it doth not

---

* Short Account of his Life, p. 4.

appear,

appear, that he contended therein out
curiosity, vain-glory, and self-conceit;
but with great humility and courtesy:
" for they who differed from him, how
mean soever, could not oblige him more,
than by pertinent objections, soberly urged,
to give him the opportunity of resolving
them : which he always did with great
simplicity and plainness of speech, without
any oftentation of learning *."

His conversation was as remote from
covetousness, as it was free from ambition.
For, when he was capable of doing it, he
supported himself by his own industry, and
refused the supplies, which benevolence and
friendship offered him ; unless, when the
necessities, brought on by imprisonment,
sickness, and the like calamities, constrained
him to avail himself of the kindness of
others. After a seven years confinement,
he was prevailed with to accept of a bed
and board from a friendly Citizen in

---

* Short Account of his Life, p. 10. and Crosby's
History of the Baptists, v. 1. p. 214.

London :

London * : and the importunities of another
induced him to do the fame, after his return
from exile in the Ifle of *Scilly*. But thefe
were exceptions to his general mode of miniftering himfelf to his wants.

He had learned to be content with a
little, and fought not more : nay, out of
that little he would contribute to the neceffities of others. His gratifications were
very moderate, for he was remarkably tem-
perate in eating, as well as in drinking.
The purity of his character was not
only moft fair and unblameable ; but, to
avoid the leaft fufpicion, he carried his
referve in his behaviour to the fex, to an
unufual (it may be called an extravagant)
degree of delicacy and caution.

He was careful to preferve juftice in his
dealings towards men, and was folicitous to
enforce and exemplify this virtue and that of
charity, as, in his opinion, effentially neceffary to falvation. And he had fuch a
lively fenfe of the obligations of humanity

* Mr. Firmin.

and kindnefs, that it was one of his leffons, which Mr. *Firmin* learnt of him, not only to relieve, but to *vifit* the fick and poor, as the beft means of adminiftering comfort to them, and of gaining an exact knowledge of their circumftances ; and as affording an opportunity to affift them by our counfel, or our intereft, more effectually than by the charity we *do* or *can* beftow upon them *.

There is another ingredient in a good and excellent character, viz. reverent, humble piety, which deferves particular mention in the delineation of Mr. *Biddle's*. " The virtues of the *devotional kind*, ob- ferves a great writer, may be fhewn by ar- guments independent of the peculiar doc- trines of revelation, to be, in their own nature, the moft truly *valuable*, as well as the moft *fublime* of all others, and to form what may be called the *key-ftone* of every truly great and heroic character †." The

* The Life of Mr. Thomas Firmin, 1698. p. 10.
† Prieftley's Letters to a Philofophical Unbeliever, Part 1. p. 211.

piety of Mr. *Biddle* was eminent. " He was, his Biographer tells us, a ſtrict obſerver himſelf, and a ſevere exactor in others, of reverence in ſpeaking of God and Christ, and holy things: ſo that he would by no means hear their names, or any ſentence of Holy Scripture, uſed vainly or lightly, much leſs any fooliſh talking, or ſcurrility." While he treated ſacred ſubjects with this reverence and gravity, he would be chearful and pleaſant, and like well that the company ſhould be ſo too. " Yet even in his common converſe, he always retained an awe of the Divine Preſence, and was ſometimes obſerved to lift up his hand ſuddenly; which thoſe that were intimate with him, knew to be an effect of a ſecret ejaculation. But in his cloſet devotions, he was wont often to proſtrate himſelf upon the ground, after the manner of our Saviour in his agony, and would commend that poſture alſo to his moſt intimate friends *."

* Short Account of his Life, p. 11.

I 3   It

It is a pertinent remark made on the excellent character, which Mr. *Biddle* supported, that the Unitarians who suffered in our country, were all of them eminent examples of piety and virtue *. It is of consequence, on every occasion that offers, to point out this; not only, as a good example can never be exhibited to view, without doing honour to religion, and leaving some good impressions on the mind;—but also to obviate the prejudices of some, even good men, who can scarcely be induced to suppose that true piety can exist, where, what they deem, great and fundamental errors, are embraced. They have been so accustomed to blend their own peculiar ideas and phraseology, with all their meditations on the Divine Being, to incorporate them with all their devout addresses to him, that they cannot conceive, how devotion can exist but under such a garb, or piety be felt but with the associations, with which they

* Mr. Lindsey's Historical View of the State of the Unitarian Doctrine, p. 503.

always

always feel it. But such persons only prove by this, how limited is their acquaintance with human characters, and how narrow are their own views of things. The principles which are the *great grounds* of devout affections, are *common* to all religious schemes: such as that *God is*, and *that He is the Rewarder of them that diligently seek him: that He hath given us eternal life, and that this life is in or by his Son* CHRIST JESUS. Into these principles may, and must all the sentiments and exercises of a pious mind be resolved, as their just cause and animating motive. To a benevolent mind it is a source of joyful reflection to believe, that the power and pleasure of these principles are and must be felt by every sincere Christian, whether *Calvinist* or *Arminian*; whether *Athanasian, Arian,* or *Socinian.* The lover of truth, especially of religious truth, cannot but possess a serious and devout mind: for he is conversant with the most serious subjects, and from them only can derive his support and consolation under the dif-

courage-

couragements and evils to which his enquiries after truth may expofe him. And if *Trinitarians* can mention a *Howe*, a *Baxter*, and a *Watts*; *Antitrinitarians* can boaft an *Emlyn*, an *Abernethy*, and a *Lardner*.

SECTION

SECTION XIII.

Conclusion —Some general reflections on Mr. Biddle's character—and on the utility of religious controversy.

SOME will be ready to hold the labours and character of Mr. *Biddle*, which we have reprefented, in low eftimation : as diftinguifhed chiefly by an exceffive attachment to religious controverfy. But the neglect or indifference, with which they themfelves treat the difcuffion of theological queftions, is not a fair and juft ftandard by which to judge of thofe whofe attention, like Mr. *Biddle*'s, hath been directed to them : for how can they be fuppofed competent to the determination of a point, on which they have beftowed no pains ? All that their opinion of its value proves, is only that fuch a direction of the thoughts and ftudies does not fuit their tafte. But ftill, still, in the great circle of human actions and purfuits, it may have its peculiar importance and ufe.

It will not be denied, that the difcovery of Truth, mathematical or philofophical, is a fuitable and valuable employment of the rational powers: and though it be not neceffary for the good of the world, that every man fhould be a Philofopher or Mathematician, yet mankind are greatly indebted to the labours, and ought to hold in high efteem, the names of thofe who have devoted their time and thoughts to fuch inveftigations: which, in innumerable inftances, are capable of being improved, and have been actually improved, to the advantage of mankind.

Why fhould its due value and praife be denied to the inveftigation of *religious* Truth? This hath a more extenfive influence, than *fcientific:* it hath a more intimate connexion with human conduct, in all the inrercourfe, and with human felicity, under all the events of life. This derives a peculiar importance, from the energy it poffeffeth,

feſſeth, to form a *moral character*; to me-
liorate the whole human race in this world;
and to train up individuals, who yield to its
power, for *eternal* PERFECTION and happineſs.

The *revelation* of religious Truth, firſt by
Moſes and the Prophets, and then by *Jeſus
Chriſt*, is a moſt ſtriking and convincing
argument of its value and importance.
Being revealed from Heaven, it becomes
an objeƈt of ſacred attention to all, to whom
it hath been communicated. There is a
merit in the improvement of any talent,
in the fulfilling of any obligation. On theſe
plain principles, the inveſtigation of religious truth hath merit: — the merit of at-
tending to what GOD hath imparted. Diligence and aſſiduity heighten this merit;
but ſufferings endured in the purſuit and
profeſſion of it, add ſtill more to it.
Probity and integrity are ineſtimable in any
courſe of life. Can they loſe their value
becauſe the principle, which calls them into
exertion, is the love of divine Truth?

Le

Let thefe confiderations be weighed ; they will affift us to appreciate the excellence and importance of fuch characters as Mr. *Biddle*. Such characters have been rendered peculiarly neceffary and ufeful, through the grofs corruptions, in which Chriftianity hath been, for ages, almoft loft. Without fuch exertions, fuch ftudies, and fuch fufferings, as mark the life of Mr. *Biddle*, no reformation from *Popery* could have taken place : or, having taken place, could have been fupported and carried on. A *Biddle*, as hath been feen, calls the attention to important queftions, throws light by difcuffion on interefting points, and awakens the fpirit of enquiry and zeal.

In aid of thefe remarks, I am induced to produce the following reflexions. " Notwithftanding the difrefpect which is occafionally fhewn towards religious controverfy, by little and illiberal minds, it is to fuch controverfies as engaged the pens of *Clarke, Hoadley* and *Sykes*, that we owe much of what is moft valuable and dear to us.

us. An affected difparagement of the feveral controverfies which have refpected religious liberty, and the improved knowledge of the Scriptures, generally indicates
an indifference to the nature and obligations of religion itfelf, or befpeaks a total
ignorance of the bleffings we derive and
enjoy from free inquiry and debate, by
means of the prefs; or is the effect of a
lamentable prejudice againft every defire
and attempt to bring all profeffing Chriftians
to abide by the plain and artlefs Gofpel of
Chrift, or, when fuch averfion to controverfy is held by well-meaning and more
candid minds, it is no other than their de-
claring their earneft defire to eftablifh the
end, while, at the fame time, they incon-
fiftently and peremptorily proteft againft
the only *means* which can effect it *."

The fentiments of the learned Bp. *Pearce*
are very pertinent here, and deferve to be
recited. " Let it be further confidered,"

---

* See the very inftructive and entertaining Memoirs
of the Life and Writings of Dr. Arthur Afhley
Sykes, by Dr. Difney, p. 365.

fays his Lordfhip, " that, if no difputes had ever been raifed in the Chriftian Church, there is great reafon to think, that lefs of truth would have been preferved in it, than there is to be found at prefent. *Cicero* tells us (Tufc. Difput. L. 2. cap. 2.) that Philofophy would not have arrived at that height of credit to which it arrived in *Greece*, if it had not received force and vigour from the controverfies and difputes which were there carried on among the learned. And fo it fares with religion : however good men may juftly diflike the methods by which difputes about religious points are too often carried on, yet we fee, that in fact ignorance of religion is no where fo grofs as where free debates about it are *not* allowed. And it is obfervable of the earlier and better ages of the Church, that when Heretics arofe, and carried fome doctrines to one extreme, it commonly was when the Church feemed inclined to bear too much towards the other extreme. Thefe Heretics then, under the guidance of Providence, caufed a *Revulfion of Humours,* as it were,

in

in the ecclefiaftical body : it brought many
back again into the right channel, and
made them ftick more clofely to the truth
than they would probably have done, if no
oppofition had been made. So that difputes
about the Chriftian Religion feem to have
contributed as much to the preferving it
pure, as the conftant motion of waters do
to the keeping them *fweet :* and if fo,
that can be no argument againft believing
Chriftianity, which has been one great caufe
of *continuing it worthy to be* believed *.

After all, it is perhaps more accurate to
defcribe Mr. BIDDLE, after his Biographer,
as a *fincere Reformer*, than a Controver-
fialift : for, befides publifhing but a few
books, he did not reply to thofe diverfe
anfwers, which were given to what he did
publifh. For this conduct feveral reafons
have been given. " Firft, that he was ve-
rily perfuaded, that truth being in itfelf
plain and fimple, efpecially what is neceffary
and very ufeful, is eafy to be apprehended

* Bp. Pearce's Sermons, V. 1. p. 386, 387.

by

by few words: it is error that feeks garnifh in many words and figures of fpeech. Again, what he did publifh, he well deliberated of; fo that he did not find in the adverfe writings, any thing of moment, which an attentive reader might not perceive already obviated; and they that attend not to the firft propofitions, will not receive benefit by replies and rejoinders. We add, that he, treading in a path, long overgrown with briars and thorns of error and fophiftry, it required vaftly greater labour and diligence to find out the way of truth, in which no Englifhman had, by any appearing footfteps, gone before him for many ages *."

To thofe who are convinced that, notwithftanding his miftakes in fome points, Mr. *Biddle* had truth on his fide in the great queftions he difcuffed, concerning the Unity of God, and the Humanity of Chrift, it will be a painful reflexion, that his opinions have made but a very flow

---

* Short Account of his Life, p. 9, 10.

2   progrefs

progress during these hundred and twenty years : at least the first hundred years of this period. The progress of truth is ever slow : for it has great difficulties to encounter from the indolence and interests of mankind ; the discovery of it is attended with a painful process : light must be let into the minds of men by degrees : and many arguments must be, one after another, laid before them ; and presented in different forms, and repeatedly renewed, before prejudices are subdued and conviction is produced. But to every sincere lover of God's truth this is a pleasing and encouraging thought : that it is GREAT, and WILL IN THE END PREVAIL.

In the mean time, it is the duty of every one to use his own best and faithful endeavours to come at the knowledge of it, and to promote it. " Let him," to use the words of the prelate just quoted, " be indifferent, if he will, to the knowledge of the several curious sciences, with which men of leisure wisely enough fill up the intervals of their time. Let him slight, if he

K   will,

will, (though I commend him not for it)
the account of what hiftory records concerning the paffages of the world, or what
Travellers or Voyagers fay concerning the
diftant parts of the Earth. In all thefe things,
his indifference, though not *praifeworthy*, is
not *criminal*, is not dangerous to the health
of his foul. But when the queftion is, "How
fhall we worfhip God aright," (it may be
as juftly faid, when it concerns the *objeƐ* of
our worfhip) " How fhall we pleafe him?
Upon what terms will he receive penitent
finners into favour? Can it be wifdom?
Can it be common fenfe, not to make a diligent and impartial inquiry? -- No man
who finds his mind entangled with doubts
and difficulties can be juftified, if he
negleƐt, as *Pilate* did, to know what the
truth is. It is his *duty* to fearch: it is his
intereft to do it; for the SAFETY of his foul
is highly concerned in it *."

* Ut fupra, p. 388, 389.

THE END,

JUST PUBLISHED,

By JOSHUA TOULMIN.

I.

The *Design of the Gospel History*, in a Sermon preached at Eſſex Chapel, London, May 11, 1788.

II.

The Conduct of the firſt Converts conſidered, in a Sermon preached at Bridport, July 10, 1788, at the Ordination of the Rev. Thomas Howe.

III.

A Letter to the Biſhops, on the Application of the Proteſtant Diſſenters, for the Repeal of the Teſt and Corporation Acts.

IV.

Propoſals for Printing by Subſcription, Price 6s. in Boards, the Hiſtory of the Town of Taunton,

ton, in the County of Somerſet ; embelliſhed with a PLAN of the TOWN, a MAP of the COUNTY ſeven Miles round it, a Perſpective View of St. MARY MAGDALEN's CHURCH, and of the NEW STREET, and the PLAN, ELEVATION, and SECTION of the HOSPITAL.

In the Preſs.

A New Edition of Sermons principally addreſſed to Youth, with two additional Diſcourſes, and ſome Prayers, Price 3s. ſewed.

N. B. After the Copies engaged for are delivered, the Price will be advanced to 3s. 6d.